Draupner's Curse

C. E. Smith

C E Smith

iUniverse, Inc.
New York   Bloomington

Draupner's Curse

Copyright © 2009 C. E. Smith

This is a work of fiction. All of the characters, names, incidents,
organizations, and dialogue in this novel are either the products
of the author's imagination or are used fictitiously.

iUniverse books may be ordered through booksellers or by contacting:

iUniverse
1663 Liberty Drive
Bloomington, IN 47403
www.iuniverse.com
1-800-Authors (1-800-288-4677)

ISBN: 978-1-4401-6799-7 (pbk)
ISBN: 978-1-4401-6797-3 (cloth)
ISBN: 978-1-4401-6798-0 (ebk)

Printed in the United States of America

iUniverse rev. date: 8/19/2009

For Monica,
with love forever

AND

Special thanks to Darik Smith
for gladly taking the time
to design the front cover

1

THE SECRET CAVE

THE SUN HAD barely risen in the east, yet the air over Colwyn Bay was already heavy and damp. It was an early indication that the unbearable humidity, which had arrived on the heels of a heat wave, was not ready to move on. So depressing was the thought of sweating through another midsummer's day that most people chose to lie in bed much longer than usual, enjoying the luxury of an air-conditioned building and taking comfort in the fact that it was Sunday and there was really no hurry to get on with their day.

But not everyone was made idle by the weather.

As fifteen year old Kyle Dunlop skipped down a dirt path that dipped steeply to the sea, a refreshing breeze brushed the coastline, rippling the surface of the tranquil bay and driving sand spirals across an isolated beach. He raised an arm to block out the blinding sun and to shield his face from the stinging sand as it suddenly blew past him. Tall and gangly, his short-sleeved shirt fluttered about narrow hips and his willowy frame seemed to sway like a trembling aspen in the gentle wind.

"I found the first coin right about here," said Kyle, brushing aside a clump of thick blonde hair so he could see where he was going and raising his voice to be heard over the sound of the terns wheeling and calling overhead. He pounded his heel in the sand and seawater oozed to the surface, promptly filling the shallow depression.

"And the other one was over there near the entrance to a cave hidden behind those rocks." He pointed to several huge granite boulders at the base of the rocky cliff that kept the restless sea at bay.

Kyle's deep blue eyes sparkled like sapphires at the thought of the two doubloons stored in a sock in the bottom drawer of his bureau and at the prospect of discovering more gold; Spanish gold. While the Spanish no longer ruled the seas, there was a time their warships prowled the Atlantic, spreading fear wherever they went and providing safe passage for vessels laden with gold. But a crushing defeat in the late sixteenth century and the cruel Atlantic took its toll, sending much of their fleet to the bottom of the sea. The ships that remained were prey for pirates, lawless men, loyal to no one, not even to their own mates.

Mistrustful captains often hoarded and hid their ill-gotten gains on an isolated island or in a deep grotto along some rocky coast; never to return. Tales abound of treasures lost and found and it was this thought alone that kept Kyle wide awake most of the night and put the glitter in his eye this morning. Stifling a yawn, he repositioned the thick coil of rope slung over his left shoulder and headed towards the granite slabs.

As Kyle moved on, eager to explore the cave, three pairs of eyeballs combed the beach with expectant eyes.

Hector Stokes, suitably nicknamed Lumpy, spotted something shiny peeking out of the sand so he quickly stuffed the remains of a chocolate cream puff into his cavernous mouth, dropped the pickaxe swinging at his side and fell to his knees, the rolls of fat around his waist spilling out of his undersized T-shirt and jiggling like tapioca pudding. In his eagerness to retrieve the object it managed to slip through his pastry covered fingers and disappear beneath the surface.

Muttering under his breath, Lumpy pawed at the sand like a dog digging for a bone; slow and methodical at first. Then fast and furious, his quivering jowls suffusing with blood as he became increasingly frustrated.

Sweating profusely beneath the relentless summer sun, he was beginning to think his efforts were in vain when his grasping fingers sensed the precious coin; an image of the two gold doubloons he had had a glimpse of the other day still crystal clear in his mind. Fearful that his prize was going to once again slip through his sweaty fingers he squeezed tightly, compressing the flat, roundish object between a fistful of sand, and stood up.

Behind greedy, porcine eyes Lumpy watched the sand disappear through the gaps between his stubby fingers and blow away in the breeze, until all that remained was the object of his desire. Unfortunately, the only thing to emerge after rubbing free and forcefully blowing on and expelling a cloying layer of dirt was an empty sand dollar shell. He gazed slack-jawed at the worthless urchin casing, remnants of the cream puff dribbling down his chin.

"Either pop it in your mouth or throw it away, Hector. Watching you drool over it is making me sick."

Megan Powers, with her slender figure, long flowing hair and delicately carved features, would have been considered pretty if not for a tendency to purse her lips, hiding flawless white teeth behind a seemingly lipless smile. Her thin lips curved upward slightly as she propped Lumpy's gaping mouth shut with a spade handle. Then she pranced away, but not before tossing her head to flick a thick coil of auburn hair out of her big brown eyes.

Lumpy's fleshy face turned brighter than his flaming red hair. "It's Lumpy, you stupid girl! When are you going to get that through your thick head?"

He tossed the shell at Megan, spraying the spot where she had been standing with bits of food and spittle. At the sound of a muffled giggle he whirled round and shot Kyle's little sister, Jan, looking on with amusement, a menacing look.

Jan was four years younger than Kyle and somewhat small for her age, with the same fair coloring and deep blue eyes as her brother, except that her hair was noticeably lighter and longer, falling over her narrow shoulders in unnatural locks of gold. Yet despite her diminutive size and seemingly docile appearance she was anything but a pushover, as anyone who ever felt the lash of her tongue could attest to. Once she caught wind of what Kyle and the others were up to, no amount of begging or pleading was going to stop her from tagging along. And when the pleas turned to threats, she countered with the most effective weapon in her arsenal; blackmail. It was amazing the effect a simple phrase like "wait until mommy hears about this" had on her thoroughly disagreeable brother. Not only did it temper his mood but it made him more willing to listen. A faint smile flickered across her elfin face as she pressed the flashlight, which she swore to guard with her life, protectively to the gaudy orange life jacket Kyle forced her to strap on, and approached the drooling behemoth.

"Don't even think about it," warned Lumpy, stopping Jan dead in her tracks.

"Whatever do you mean?" said Jan innocently.

Not about to be fooled by this pretence of innocence Lumpy eyed her from under beetling brows. "You know exactly what I mean."

"I most certainly do not," sniffed Jan. "Now, if you don't mind, I would like to proceed." She stiffened her narrow shoulders and raised her head, returning his hostile look.

"Go ahead," said Lumpy, stepping aside and waving her on. "It's not as if I'm stopping you."

Jan sniffed again. Then she proceeded to boldly step around the behemoth.

If there is one thing Lumpy had learned over the years it was to never trust Jan. He kept this thought in mind, wisely waiting until she was several paces away, beyond the perceived danger zone, before bending over to retrieve the pickaxe. However, no sooner had he gripped the handle than the little minx spun round and darted towards him, heaving her diminutive frame at his bowed figure and hollering.

"Hector! Hector! Hector!"

The confidence Jan possessed when she first eyed the tempting target, like the thrill of the moment, vanished the instant she made contact. Not only did she fail to send Lumpy sprawling to the ground as envisioned, but she actually bounced off him, falling flat on her back and winding herself in the process.

A feeling of helplessness washed over her like a wave as she sought to refill her lungs. But before she drew her first breath Lumpy was hovering over her, his fat mug convulsed with rage. She screamed loud enough to wake up the dead. Then her instincts took over and, as Lumpy leaned over to wring her scrawny neck, she grabbed a fistful of sand and threw it in his face. Some of it struck his beady eyes.

Lumpy clawed at the sand in his eyes but the harder he scraped the more ingrained the particles became, irritating his eyes further and making it increasingly difficult to see. Through watery eyes he saw Jan roll onto her stomach and scrabble to her feet. He took a swipe at the fuzzy image but all he felt was air. He roared to show his displeasure.

Jan was so relieved to escape with all her limbs intact that she didn't look back until she was standing amongst the granite boulders, safely next to Kyle and Megan. Even then, it took her a moment to catch her breath and regain her composure. It was only when she glanced at Megan and noticed that the other girl was having trouble holding a straight face that she burst out laughing. Their peals of laughter rang out across the sandy beach, echoing off the rocky precipice that held back the sea at high tide.

Although Kyle had watched with amusement, it was evident early on that Jan was going to be more of a nuisance than usual, especially if Megan continued to encourage her. However, as much as he wanted to tell her to get lost he knew it was out of the question. The first thing she would do is run straight to their mother and snitch on him. And then he would never get to explore the cave. Never get to find the treasure. On the other hand, if he allowed her to accompany them and something terrible happened to her he would really be in trouble. Perhaps he could ask her to stay behind and keep watch, while Megan and Lumpy went with him to conduct a search. He could always deal with his mother after he found more coins; after he found the pirate's hoard.

"Are you sure you don't want to stay here while we look around inside?" pleaded Kyle. "It could be dangerous. That's why mom and dad told us to stay away from these caves." His eyes begged her to say yes.

Jan slipped through a narrow opening between two slabs of granite almost twice her size and peered at the cave, searching for an answer in the darkness beyond and backing away suddenly when she heard something moving about inside. However, whatever trepidation she may have had quickly vanished when she saw Lumpy lumbering towards her clenching his fists. His face was flushed and his breath came in huge gulps, puffing out through his thick nostrils in the manner of a bull about to charge.

"I don't care how dangerous it is," said Jan. "I'd rather take a chance on whatever is lurking in there than let him get his grubby hands on me."

"Have it your way," said Kyle tersely. "Only don't come crying to me if you get scared."

Kyle ripped the flashlight out of Jan's hand, almost wrenching her shoulder from its socket. Then he squeezed through the granite slabs and stormed inside the cave.

Jan paused, opened her mouth as if to say something, took one look at Lumpy, decided against it and followed her ill-tempered brother.

Afraid of what might happen if Lumpy and Jan got too close to each other, Megan rushed in after Jan. Lumpy lowered his outstretched hands and fell in step behind Megan, but not before snorting to blow off some steam.

A few paces beyond the sunbathed entrance Kyle clicked on the flashlight. In its beam the floor of the cave came to life as hundreds of ghost crabs scuttled about in a panic to escape the glow. While some of the crustaceans vanished by burrowing beneath a thin layer of pebbles, others sought refuge behind a concealing rock or in the shadows just beyond the illuminating beam. Now and again one of the creatures would cross their path and a loud crunch would break the near silence of the cave.

Jan was having second thoughts the moment she set eyes on the denizens of the cave but she was too stubborn to admit it. And although she managed to suppress a scream that rose in her throat when she first saw the crabs, she was unable to hide her fear when one of the creatures scuttled around Kyle and side-stepped directly into her path. She shrieked at the sound of the carapace snapping and cracking underfoot. The thought of its guts plastered to the bottom of her shoe made her stomach churn.

"What's the matter?" jeered Lumpy. "Is the whittle girl afraid of the dark?"

"Drop dead, Lumpy!" said Megan.

To dispel some of her own fears Megan took hold of Jan's hand and gave it a reassuring squeeze.

"If it's any consolation, Jan, I don't like them either. They remind me a lot of spiders."

She gave an involuntary shiver as a rather large crustacean clicked its claws at her in annoyance and clambered over her outstretched foot.

Well, at least she didn't call me Hector, Lumpy thought to himself.

In the darkness that surrounded them the cave seemed much larger than it really was, so it came as somewhat of a surprise when they suddenly reached the end. Fortunately, there were two passable tunnels to explore; one leading off to the left and the other one extending at a slight angle to the right. Kyle paused, probing each passage with the light. The tunnel on the left appeared more promising, if only because it was wider, two yards across and just as high, so he followed his instincts and started down it. The others joined him, leaving behind the ghost crabs and the lulling rhythm of the sea.

Jagged, rib-like ridges running down the walls of the passage gave the impression they were walking through the fossilized remains of a prehistoric beast, entombed for millions of years in a sedimentary grave; petrified by the sands of time and only recently exposed by the constant pounding of the sea.

Kyle kept his eyes fixed on the beam of light as it scanned the pebbly floor. But with so much gravel lying about he knew it was like looking for a needle in a haystack. He crossed his fingers, hoping his luck would hold and praying the treasure was real and not just a figment of his wild imagination. An imagination nurtured on a steady diet of pirate tales, fuelled by the likes of Blackbeard, Captain Hook and Long John Silver.

Despite the cool, damp feel of the cave, Megan found herself breaking out in a cold sweat. The fear that gripped her whenever she waded through a sea of people in a crowded mall was no different and no less intense. Yet, where the crowd would bend and yield to her touch, the walls of the tunnel were solid, immovable. And the fact that the narrow passage was beginning to close in on her only served to intensify the fear. She must have slowed down without being aware of it because Lumpy bumped into her.

"Pick up the pace or get out of the way," said Lumpy, jabbing Megan in the back.

One whiff of Lumpy's warm, fetid breath was enough to urge Megan on.

It wasn't long after Lumpy growled in Megan's ear that they were all forced to stop as the tunnel branched to the left and right, then ended abruptly in an impassable wall of rock.

"Damn!"

Kyle didn't think anyone would hear him curse but then, he hadn't counted on the stone chamber amplifying his voice.

Shocked, Jan clicked her tongue and drew in a mouthful of air. "Just wait until mommy hears what you said."

"She won't know unless you tell her," said Megan.

"Yeah, you little snitch." The disdain in Lumpy's voice spilled over to his features as he sneered at Jan.

Heedless of the consequences Jan poked out her tongue. She ducked behind Megan when Lumpy snarled and moved menacingly towards her.

Kyle let out an exasperated sigh.

"Try to ignore her, Lumpy. She'll just keep pestering you if you don't." He frowned severely at Jan.

"Not if you let me wring her neck," said Lumpy, leering at Jan as he imagined wrapping his outstretched hands around her scrawny neck.

A malicious grin curled the corner of Kyle's mouth.

"I'd like to let you, but I don't think it would please my parents. So let's stop wasting time and go check out that other tunnel."

"Do we have to?" grumbled Megan. "The air is so stale in here I can barely breathe, and just look what the dampness is doing to my hair."

She yanked on a long, silky coil, making her natural wavy hair appear much straighter than it actually was.

"That's so typical of you, Megan," said Lumpy critically. "We're supposed to be looking for treasure and the only thing you can think about is your stupid hair."

"Well, at least I don't always think about my stomach."

"You wouldn't be so skinny if you did."

"I really don't care if you two stand there and argue all day," said Kyle in a tired voice. But do me a favor—since I can't go through you—move out of the way so I can get by."

Kyle didn't wait for Lumpy and Megan to move. Instead, he squeezed past them and proceeded to retrace his steps.

The others fell silent and followed.

•   •   •   •

Once again they found themselves in the main cavern, and while Kyle, Lumpy and Jan headed straight for the other passage, Megan paused halfway there, reluctant to go any further.

As much as she wanted to believe that there was more gold to be found, there was a cloud of doubt hanging over her that was hard to dispel. Two coins do not make a treasure, even though Kyle was convinced otherwise. It was this sense of uncertainty that kept urging her to sneak away before anyone noticed she was missing. She watched Kyle disappear inside the tunnel and imagined how easy it would be to escape while everyone's back was turned. With this thought in mind, she turned about and began creeping towards the exit.

"What are you doing?" said Lumpy in a booming voice.

Megan almost jumped out of her skin.

Spinning round, she saw Lumpy's fat head poking out of the tunnel. He threw her a bemused look.

"Well?"

For a moment Megan's mind went blank and she was unable to think clearly. However, she soon composed herself and came up with a plausible explanation.

"If you must know, I was about to remove my shoe and get rid of a pebble that's bothering me almost as much as you." Using the shovel for balance, she raised her left leg and pulled off her shoe.

Lumpy shook his head and muttered something that contained the words "stupid" and "girls". Then he disappeared, leaving Megan to hop around in the dark.

Once Megan was finally alone and it was eerily dark and quiet she suddenly became aware of her surroundings. And the thought of standing in a gloomy damp cave, sharing the same space with Lord knows how many creepy-crawlies made the narrow passage seem all that more inviting. In fact, the decision to rejoin the others was made long before several loud clicks sent her screaming through the tunnel.

It only took Megan a few seconds to catch up to the others but when Kyle pointed the flashlight at her she was leaning on the shovel, puffing like she had just run the mile in record time. He noticed she was balancing herself on one foot. Perhaps that was because the other foot was sorely in need of something other than a dirty pink sock. She must have realized he was staring at the stocking because she quickly covered it with a blue sneaker. Her hands were trembling as she knotted the laces.

"What happened to you?" said Kyle, shining the beam of light on her ashen face. "You look like you saw a ghost."

"Not saw. Heard," said Megan. "Those horrible little creatures tried to make a meal out of me."

Her eyebrows edged upward when she noticed there was a cave-in further along the passage.

Lumpy snorted mockingly. "Some meal you would make. A chicken leg has more meat on it than you."

Megan gave Lumpy a sharp look. "At least I'm not a bloated, overstuffed pig like you!"

"Hey!" hollered Lumpy, loud enough to shake loose some fragments of the tunnel that spilled into the air. "You watch who you're calling a pig!"

Lumpy edged closer to Megan but Kyle put a restraining hand on his shoulder.

"Save your strength. You're going to need it to get through that." Kyle waved the flashlight at a mound of rocks that rose almost to the roof of the tunnel.

Megan groaned. "Are you crazy? You can't possibly move all those rocks."

Kyle was disappointed by this latest setback, however he was careful not to let his frustration show.

"I don't intend to. If we shift some of those rocks at the top we should be able to make a hole large enough to crawl through."

At a loss for words, Megan dropped her jaw and gawked at the seemingly impenetrable obstacle.

Lumpy eyed Megan's gaping jaw and couldn't wait to shut her chops, just like she had done to him back at the beach. Lunging forward, he grasped the handle of the shovel, jerking it upwards and closing her mouth. Then he released his grip, waddled over to the rock pile, and started to tear into it with the pickaxe, all the while whistling, "Hi-ho. Hi-ho. It's off to work we go—"

With the ghost of a smile, Kyle dropped the coiled rope at Megan's feet and exchanged the flashlight for the shovel.

"Here, make yourself useful," he said.

Kyle shifted Megan's hand to make sure the beam of light illuminated the rock pile before departing to join Lumpy. As he strolled away Megan stabbed him with her eyes.

Jan noticed the daggers and she knew exactly what was going through Megan's mind. Boys! Stubborn. Pig-headed. Rude. Crude. Pushy. Bossy. It never ceased to amaze her how many adjectives were reserved entirely for boys. And topping the list was—stupid! Shaking her head in disbelief, she crossed her arms in front and leaned back against the hard stone wall; a casual observer to the spectacle about to unfold.

The noise was deafening—more so for Kyle and Lumpy since they weren't able to cover their ears to deaden the sound.

Even so, Megan and Jan could still hear and feel every blow of the pickaxe, every scrape of the shovel. It felt as though they were standing in a war zone, being bombarded from all sides. Any moment one of the shells would find its target and put them out of their misery. They pulled their shirts up over their noses so they didn't have to breathe in the cloying dust and closed their eyes, hoping that the end would come soon.

The din went on for almost an hour and, when it was over and the air had cleared somewhat, the boys could be seen standing in a pile of rubble. Directly behind them was a cavity, chest high and barely large enough to accommodate Lumpy's large girth. A cloud of dust caught in a beam of light floated through space near the opening, inviting them to step inside.

Kyle dropped the shovel and, with the palm of his hand, he mopped at the sheen of sweat on his brow. "That should do it," he said, panting and sizing up the hole.

He rubbed at a nagging itch, smearing his face with grime and depositing a clod of dirt on the tip of his nose. It hung there, glistening like an inflamed pimple.

"It better," said Lumpy, his massive chest heaving, "because I'm not moving from this spot."

Ragged with exertion, Lumpy leaned on the pickaxe, rivers of sweat coursing through his greasy hair and cascading to the ground. Perspiration stains radiated outward from both armpits, soaking up the dirt he had picked up along the way and turning his white T-shirt a most unappealing sludge color.

Repelled by the sight, Megan and Jan curled their lips in disgust and looked the other way.

Lumpy observed their reaction out of the corner of his eye and his face split into a wide grin.

Although Kyle knew what was going to happen next, he just had enough time to throw up his hands in defense; but even then he wasn't able to completely avoid the deluge that followed when Lumpy shook his head like a wet shaggy mutt, spraying the air with sweat and drenching everything in sight.

Megan and Jan jumped up and down, shrieking horribly and waving their arms about like a traffic controller having an epileptic fit. They swept at their hair, their faces, their necks, all over their befouled bodies, in an attempt to brush away the fallout and to avoid contamination.

"Wow! Did that ever feel good," said Lumpy.

He ran a dirty hand through his sopping red hair so that it was standing up in damp locks, rather than plastered flat to his head.

"You're disgusting," said Megan.

Lumpy belched loudly in agreement.

Normally, Kyle would have been amused but, with the situation at home going from bad to worse, he was finding it more and more difficult to listen to Megan and Lumpy. So as their adolescent bickering continued, he was seriously regretting the decision to let them in on his secret. However, since he had confided in them, the only thing he could do now was show his displeasure by venting and throwing them a dark look.

"If you two can't find anything else to do, then you might as well go home," said Kyle severely. "And take her with you."

He pointed an accusatory finger at Jan, giving the impression that she was to blame for Megan and Lumpy's behavior.

"Don't get mad at me," said Jan, stiffening her shoulders, puffing out her chest and crossing her arms across the orange life preserver. "He's the one who started it." She eyed Lumpy with disdain.

Lumpy grinned unashamedly. "I was only trying to have some fun."

"And now that you've succeeded," said Kyle tartly, "perhaps you can *try* harder to be more serious. Or have you forgotten why we're here?"

Kyle saw the flash of guilt on Lumpy's face and he knew he had struck a chord.

"That's better. Now, if you three don't mind, I'd like to see what's on the other side of this rock pile."

Upon that announcement, Kyle snatched the flashlight out of Megan's hand and moved towards the opening, leaving the others behind in the dark. The last thing he heard as he slipped through the gap was a menacing growl cut short by a shrill, somewhat hysterical voice. They were at it again but at least now he didn't have to listen to them.

•　　　•　　　•　　　•

Over the years erosion, caused by the constant ebb and flow of the sea, had carved the cave and the adjoining passages out of solid rock. But now this same force of nature was working just as hard to destroy what it had once created. Everywhere, slabs of granite lay strewn about, the end result of countless tides undermining the structure by scraping away the sandstone base and exposing the harder igneous rock. As the roof and walls crumbled under the weight, the tunnel was reduced to little more than a crawl space. Kyle cursed as he banged his forehead, taking some solace in the fact that Jan wasn't around to reproach him.

To avoid knocking himself senseless he crouched low to the ground, crawling along on his forearms and knees. As the oppressive heat and suffocating air sapped him of his strength, the all encompassing rocks punished him entirely. Soon, he was sure he had bruises on his bruises, and the pain in his arms and legs became so unbearable it was hard to fight back the tears. He had half a mind to turn around, if that was possible, when the first sign he was on the right track appeared before his cloudy eyes.

He palmed the coin.

Not surprisingly, it was coated in a thick layer of dirt, much like the other two coins he had found. Recalling how the gold sparkled like new shortly after immersing the coins in a homemade concoction corrosive enough to strip the flesh off a bone, he put this latest discovery in his pocket. Then, he brushed aside some of the surrounding dirt and debris just in case there were more coins to be found. But what his probing hand uncovered next chilled him to the bone.

Stifling a scream, he shifted a boulder to hide the grim discovery; a partially buried human skull that peered at him through empty eye sockets.

Once the pounding in his chest subsided he crept forward, sweeping the surface, expecting to uncover bits and pieces of the skeleton. He didn't see any more bones or coins lying about, so he moved on.

He managed to crawl several more feet when the floor of the tunnel suddenly fell out from under him. Fortunately, he was moving so slow he caught himself before he tumbled over the edge, into the darkness below. An offensive odor assailed his nostrils, causing him to gag.

After recovering from the shock and the stench, he shined the light down and peered over the edge of the precipice. The void turned out to be a vast, subterranean cave, about ten feet lower than and twice that distance higher than the level of the crawl space. The walls were sheer, straight up and down.

Although the opposite wall was barely visible, he was able to make out a narrow ledge, clinging precariously to the vertical surface. The base of the ledge must have eroded long ago, leaving it suspended in the still air a few feet off the ground. But Kyle wasn't interested in this or any of the more salient features of the underground grotto. All he cared about was getting closer to the hanging ledge to take a better look at the manmade object sitting amongst the rubble.

Without a rope to clamber down on he had no choice but to lean forward as far as possible and stretch outward with the flashlight. As he tried to hold the beam of light steady, he could feel sweat running down his forearm, getting between his fingers and the torch. He wiggled his fingers to get a better grip, letting the flashlight slip, but not before he had time to convince himself that what he saw was real.

He wanted to leap in the air and celebrate but there was no room in the crawlspace to do so. Instead, he backed away, performed a difficult about-face, and proceeded to retrace his steps, anxious to share the thrilling news with the others.

THE PIRATE'S HOARD

2

THE SILENCE THAT greeted Kyle when he poked his head out of the crawlspace was unnerving, leading him to believe that Lumpy, Megan and Jan had deserted him. He really couldn't blame them. It must have been dreadfully boring sitting in the dark with nothing better to do than get under each others' skin. He was praying they had the good sense to leave the rope behind when he illuminated the tunnel and saw Lumpy sitting with his back against the wall, idly tossing a pebble in the air. His lips were moving but no sound was coming out of his mouth.

Distracted by the beam of light, Lumpy dropped the stone. "Rats! Now I'll have to start over." He chose another pebble from the large number at his disposal and began throwing it up and catching it, as if he had nothing else better to do.

Megan and Jan were huddled together, further along the opposite wall. While Jan looked tired, Megan appeared agitated. She fixed Kyle with a frosty glare and said, "So, can we get out of here now?"

"You can leave any time you want," said Kyle matching her chilly tone. "But do me a favor. Take her with you." He waved the flashlight at Jan. The younger girl yawned heavily, her sleepy eyes glistening in the artificial light. "I wouldn't want her to miss her afternoon nap."

Jan raised an arm to shield her eyes from the blinding light. "Hey, I'm not tired—just bored. How much longer do we have to sit here doing nothing?"

"Like I said," Kyle reminded her. "You two can leave any time."

"Why don't we all call it a day?" suggested Lumpy, pitching aside the pebble and rising with a grimace. "My stomach says it's lunch time." He rubbed his jiggly belly.

"That's where all the growling was coming from," said Megan wryly. "And I thought you were trying to scare us."

Lumpy gave a dry, humorless laugh. "Very funny."

"Forget about your stomach," said Kyle. "When I tell you what I saw you'll forget all about food."

Lumpy regarded Kyle strangely. "What could possibly be more important than food?"

"Treasure."

"What!" said Jan, springing lively to her feet. "There's no way I'm going home now, no matter what you say."

Megan was skeptical. "I don't believe it. Not until I see it with my own eyes."

"You'll see it soon enough," said Kyle, his face darkening in a frown. "And when you do you'll be sorry you ever doubted me."

Suddenly becoming animated, Kyle turned to Lumpy and added, "Didn't I tell you when I found those two coins there had to be more—a lot more? All I had to do was look in the right place, and there it was, right in front of my nose."

"The treasure?" wondered Lumpy.

"No. This."

Kyle reached into his pocket and pulled out the coin he had found. He waved it at Lumpy, and then poked it in Megan's face.

"That!" said Megan. "It looks like a worthless piece of limestone."

"So did the other two coins but you saw what they looked like after I cleaned them both up."

Kyle slipped the coin back in his pocket.

Megan remained doubtful. "So you found another coin. Big deal."

As much as he hated to admit it, Lumpy had to agree.

"Megan's right, you know. We could look all day and not find another thing."

Kyle laughed. "Why would I want to do that when I already know where it is?"

Megan sighed. Her mouth popped open as if she was going to say something but before she could utter another word Kyle continued.

"All I need is a rope so I can get my hands on the chest."

He probed the floor with a beam of light and focused on the coiled rope. "Ah! There it is."

"What chest?" Lumpy and Jan chorused.

Kyle moved towards the rope.

"The treasure chest I was going to tell you about. But I never did get around to it. Did I?"

He threw Megan an admonishing look.

Lumpy lunged forward and knocked Kyle aside.

"I'll get that," he said, scooping up the rope.

As he gripped the rope tightly, he draped his free arm over Kyle's shoulders and said, "Lead the way, buddy, old pal and, while you're at it, you might as well tell me about this treasure chest of ours."

There was a sense of excitement in the air as Lumpy accompanied Kyle to the opening. Megan and Jan followed close behind giggling and twittering to beat the band now that it was evident they weren't chasing a false dream.

●   ●   ●   ●

Kyle shot through the crawlspace the second time around, arriving at the other end on a wave of adrenalin. And while he paused and waited for Lumpy, Megan and Jan to catch up, he let his mind wander.

Although he had a good idea of what he was going to spend most of his share of the gold on, he couldn't imagine what to do with the rest of it until he knew precisely how many coins there were inside the chest. Of course, he wouldn't know that until he got a closer look. He was thinking about how wonderful it would be to run his fingers through all that gold when he sensed someone breathing down his neck.

"Why did you stop?" said Lumpy.

Kyle tilted the flashlight down, emphasizing the sheer drop just a foot or so away.

Lumpy whistled. "Now I know why you wanted the rope."

"Exactly," said Kyle. "So back up a bit so I can roll that boulder—" He aimed the beam of light at a huge slab of rock to his right. "—into this depression I'm kneeling on."

As Lumpy obeyed, Kyle backed out of the shallow hollow. Then he laid the rope down, stringing one end across the depression and rolling the boulder, which was rounded for the most part, over it. He was careful to leave enough rope on the one side of the boulder to be able to fasten it to the rock. This he promptly did once the boulder was shifted into position. Only when he was satisfied that the boulder was firmly in place and the rope was securely fastened to it did he fling the rest of the line over the edge and begin his descent.

The wall of the cavern was smooth and perilously slick so Kyle's feet slipped each time he made contact, transferring the bulk of his weight to his arms and forcing him to grip the coarse rope so hard he could feel it digging into the flesh. A pungent odor permeated the air and, for a moment, he thought his hands were burning, but it was only the over-powering stench of the cave. He coughed, the bile rising in his throat, and he was just able to suppress the urge to vomit when he reached the bottom.

He thought he was planting his feet on solid ground but the surface was so slimy he lost his footing and slipped. Sploosh! If he didn't know better he could have sworn he stepped on a cow patty. The sudden tug on the rope, which was still fused to his hands, must have jerked the anchor rock free because he felt the rope fall weightlessly in his hands; but only momentarily. He heard a loud grunt overhead and, before any damage was done, the slack was taken up and the rope had once again gone taut.

"Hey! What are you doing down there?" shouted Lumpy.

His booming voice echoed off the walls of the cavern.

Through the echoes Kyle heard a squeak. He directed the beam of light upward and noticed that the cave was home to hundreds, if not, thousands of bats, clinging upside down to the giant stalactites that adorned the roof of the cavern. He told himself to watch where he stepped.

"Come on down, Lumpy," said Kyle. "But watch your step when you get to the bottom. There's bat dung everywhere and it's as slick as ice."

Kyle lit the way as Lumpy descended, grimacing at the sound of some pebbles spilling over the edge. For a moment he didn't think the boulder would remain in place but eventually Lumpy reached the bottom safely.

Breathing a sigh of relief, Kyle pointed the flashlight at the opening and said, "You're next, Jan."

Jan poked her head out and gagged, just as Kyle had when he caught his first whiff of the fetid air.

"What's that horrible smell?" she said, staring accusingly at Lumpy.

"Don't look at me," said Lumpy, appearing offended.

In answer to Jan's question Kyle illuminated the roof of the cavern.

"Bats."

At first Jan noticed the stalactites but nothing else. However, as her eyes grew more accustomed to the lighting she began to make out individual shapes, clustered around the limestone icicles. She might have thought the elongated forms were nothing more than a natural extension of the limestone formations, if only one of the bats hadn't stirred. Tilting back its fuzzy little head, the creature smirked and stared at her through sleepy eyes.

Jan had heard enough horror stories about bats to make her terrified of the creatures. Instinctively, she covered her head and screamed.

It was a piercing sound that had a ripple effect in the vast cavern. Everywhere, wings flapped and tiny voices squeaked as the disturbance was noted, evaluated and dismissed for what it was; nothing but a nuisance. Foreseeing no immediate threat to their well-being, all but one of the bats returned to their slumber.

The lone holdout was the same creature that had startled Jan. Still half asleep, the drowsy bat stretched out its leathery wings and yawned, opening its mouth wide to reveal a little pink tongue and a double row of tiny, jagged teeth. Then, it retracted its wings, bent over so that its rear end was pointing downward and defecated.

Jan watched with growing delight as the glistening projectile spun through the air several times and landed with a splat on Lumpy's shoulder.

"Stupid thing," said Lumpy.

He quickly scanned the floor of the cavern to see if he could find something to toss back at the bat. Fortunately, there was a good sized stone within easy reach but, as he leaned back to hurl it at the boorish creature, Kyle put a restraining hand on his arm.

"I wouldn't do that if I were you," said Kyle. "You just saw the mess one of those things can make. I can only image what would happen if you disturbed the others."

Lumpy eyed the greenish lump on his shoulder and the slick path it was making down the front of his shirt. Glowering at the bat, he lowered his arm and wisely dropped the stone.

Satisfied, the bat resumed a restful pose and closed its eyes, the corners of its mouth curling upward in what appeared to be a contented smile.

Jan slid effortlessly down the rope, somewhat less fearful of the bats now that she saw how cute they actually were.

As soon as Jan touched the ground Megan began her descent, driven by the fear that gripped her. As much as she loathed bats, or anything else that lurked in the night, she hated being confined in the dark, airless, crawlspace even more. Kyle swung the flashlight away from Megan so the others couldn't see the look of terror on her face, and shone it on the treasure chest.

He was pleased to see that the chest had not been disturbed. Not since he last set eyes on it. Not for three or four centuries perhaps, since that fateful day when one man's misfortune became another man's destiny. As he drew closer to the ledge and his destiny, the air around him grew heavy and cold; as if the spirit of the doomed pirate whose skull he had discovered was hovering nearby, stubbornly guarding the treasure.

For a moment he felt trapped by the ghost's damp, icy grip. Then the feeling passed and he was free to proceed, as though the spirit he imagined quitted this world, knowing the treasure was lost. He stepped onto the ledge, leaving Megan, Lumpy and Jan behind, in the shadows, to stare incredulously at the chest.

The ledge, loosened by the ravages of time, groaned under Kyle's weight. Along the wall joint, pieces of the brittle rock cracked and chipped off, disappearing through deep cracks in the seam. He paused—waiting—listening. But when nothing further happened he proceeded more cautiously over to the chest.

At first he saw what he wanted to see—diamonds and pearls—emeralds and rubies—all heaped atop a mound of gold doubloons. Then, to his dismay, he realized it was just an illusion, deceptively conjured in his mind's eye. He stood in stunned silence, unable to move, unable to speak, mesmerized by a mass of glittering crystals that must have fallen from the roof of the cavern after being scraped loose by countless clawed feet. Flotsam and jetsam, floating amid an endless sea of bat dung.

Kyle hadn't come this far to go away empty-handed so, instead of graciously accepting defeat, he plunged one hand in the dung heap and felt around. However, nothing his probing fingers touched seemed to feel just right. He dug deeper, dipping his arm in up to the elbow and running his hand along the bottom of the chest. But there was still no sign of anything else inside other than rocks and warm, mushy bat dung. With a sense of hopelessness, he eased out his slime-covered arm.

The foul smelling dung clung to him, molding his fist into a viscous mallet that was almost too heavy to lift. He flicked his wrist and a particularly large glob of dung shot through the air, smacked against the wall and slopped onto the ledge, dislodging a piece of the brittle joint. As the broken chunk of rock slipped through a gap between the wall and the ledge, Kyle turned to walk away, his slouched shoulders and a pained expression revealing the disappointment that he felt.

He made it halfway to the lip of the ledge when a loud crack caused him to stop dead in his tracks, but by then it was too late; the damage was done. Suddenly, he felt the ledge tremble beneath his feet. A moment later it broke away from the wall and crashed with a resounding thud to the ground.

The last thing Jan saw before everything went dark was Kyle leaping in the air and vanishing in a cloud of dust.

"Kyle!" she cried.

The resulting boom sent shock waves through the cavern, startling the bats and sending them airborne in a panic. Jan listened for Kyle but the sound of the bats was deafening. In the end she had to cover her ears like Megan and Lumpy, and wait for the tempest of screeching bats and droppings to pass.

Jan knew the storm had passed when the wind gusting from so

many flapping wings subsided and no more bat dung fell on her head. However, no sooner had she uncovered her ears than she was flooded by light.

"You look terrible," said Kyle, probing her sopping wet hair with the flashlight.

"You don't look so good yourself," said Jan, squinting through the brilliant beam and eying with concern an ugly gash over Kyle's left eye.

A clump of loose skin made the cut look much worse than it really was. Kyle knew Jan was squeamish when it came to blood, so he drew her attention away from the gash by lowering the flashlight and saying, "What happened to Megan and Lumpy?"

"We're over here," Lumpy called out in the dark.

Kyle swept the cavern with light but he had to wait for Lumpy to step into the beam's path before his hulking frame came into view. He noticed Megan standing in the shadows next to Lumpy, frantically trying to dig the bat dung out of her hair.

"I'll have to wash my hair for a week," said Megan in her typical whiny voice. "And that's just to get rid of the stench."

"I don't know," said Lumpy. "It smells better than that perfume you always douse on."

Megan flicked her wrists, splattering Lumpy with dung.

Before things could get totally out of hand Kyle distracted them.

"Listen!" he said, holding a finger up to his lips and cocking his head to one side.

Surprisingly, Megan and Lumpy paused to listen. At first they didn't hear anything. Then the sound of water dripping in echoing plops caught their ears. They held their breath in anticipation as the dripping became more and more pronounced.

Foreseeing the sea's arrival long before it roared through the crawlspace and burst through the opening, Kyle probed the cavern with the flashlight, searching for another exit. He was unable to find one.

"What are we going to do?" screeched Megan.

"Run!" shouted Kyle.

"Where?" cried Megan.

The tears running down her cheeks flowed almost as freely as the seawater spilling out of the crawlspace.

Kyle could feel the water tugging on his calves, racing by him on a deliberate course.

"That way," he said, directing the beam of light between Megan and Lumpy. "If we're lucky, there might be another way out up ahead."

No sooner had the words left his mouth than a wall of water slammed against him. He slipped on the slick surface and his knees buckled as he struggled to maintain his footing and prevent being carried away by the swelling waves.

The sudden rush of seawater indicated there was a breach in the wall upstream. Soon the entire cavern was going to be underwater, along with anyone trapped inside; unless, of course, they could make their way downstream and find another tunnel—one that wasn't already submerged. Kyle steadied himself by crouching lower and putting most of his weight on his legs. Then he looked around anxiously for Jan.

He spotted the orange life jacket and yelled out to Jan, but she made the mistake of turning to face him while balancing on one leg. One moment she was standing next to him. The next moment she was being swept away by the rising tide.

"Jan!"

Kyle reached for Jan's outstretched hand but all he could sense was water and the chilling scream that erupted from her lungs as she drifted past him.

There was no time to lose. Kyle dove into the torrent and began thrashing at the choppy water, trying desperately to catch up to the bobbing life jacket. In a beam of light that was visible one moment and nowhere to be seen the next, when the hand that gripped the flashlight was thrust beneath the surface on alternating strokes, Kyle caught a brief glimpse of Lumpy and Megan. They were walking arm in arm, making their way slowly downstream.

Each time Kyle closed in on the life jacket an unexpected wave tossed it aside and widened the gap. He thought he was never going to reach Jan when, all of a sudden, a giant swell lifted him out of the water and practically hurled him on top of her. As he reached for the life jacket a loose strap whipped through the air and slapped him in the face.

For a moment the only thing he could feel was the strap's stinging bite. Then his left shoulder slammed against the cavern wall and pain, so agonizing he almost passed out, shot down his arm. Numbed by the pain, his left arm went limp.

With no chance of reaching Jan now, Kyle stopped struggling and let the surging water carry him away.

3
MIDGARD

TIME AND AGAIN Kyle succumbed to fatigue and slipped beneath the surface of the water, but somehow he always managed to find the strength to fight his way to the top, breaking free of the suffocating sea, swallowing great gulps of air.

At one point he broke through the surface and found himself being swept towards an outcrop of solid rock running perpendicular to the cavern wall. Moments before he hit the protrusion he threw out his aching left arm to cushion the blow. He let out an anguished scream and a disappointed groan when his right hand slammed into the rock wall, as well, knocking the flashlight out of his clenched fist. He watched in stunned silence as the comforting glow grew dimmer and dimmer, and was eventually swallowed up by the water.

As the current pulled him along, he thrashed at the water with one hand and felt for something to cling onto and impede his progress with the other. Unfortunately, the outcrop was as smooth as glass. He clawed at it but to no avail and, while his fingers grated on solid rock, the torrent eventually directed him around the obstacle, into open water once again.

Before long, the walls of the cavern closed in on him until he could almost reach out and touch both sides. Eventually the space he was confined to became extremely cramped, not much bigger than the crawlspace, but tubular in shape and more slick; without all those treacherous rocks lying about to rip and tear at his flesh. And the downward slope, which he never really considered until now, suddenly became more pronounced. If he didn't know any better he might have thought he was on a giant waterslide. And the sudden, sharp dip was just another part of the ride. He tried to hold on to this thought as his body zoomed through the pitch-dark tunnel, on a seemingly endless downward course.

In the blackness that surrounded him he lost all track of time and space. So what seemed like an hour were really only a few minutes, from the moment he dove in the water in a vain attempt to rescue Jan, to the point where gravity, not water, was the catalyst that propelled him forward.

Surprisingly, Kyle was more relaxed than at any other point. Perhaps it had something to do with the feeling that much of the danger had passed, and it was now time to sit back and enjoy the ride; if only that was possible.

The calm he felt gave him time to reflect, and with all the thoughts swirling around inside his head, his concern for Jan was foremost in his mind. He knew she was still out there, alone and terrified just like him. He just didn't know how far away from him she actually was. Maybe if she heard his voice it would comfort her to know that he had not given up. That he was still trying to reach her. He inhaled deeply, expecting the next thing he was going to hear would be the sound of his own voice. But before he was able to call out to Jan, the floor of the waterslide seemed to fall out from under him and he found himself holding onto his breath as he plunged down a deafening waterfall.

Kyle hit the foaming water and sank like an anchor, the roar of the cataract still ringing in his ears. He told himself to remain calm and not give in to fear; to conserve his strength until the storm swirling around him had time to pass and give way to calmer waters. Then he felt his chest tightening and he knew there was no time to waste. He had to break for the surface now, or be trapped forever in the bubbling, churning water.

Panic-stricken, he pumped his arms and legs, twisting and turning in a frantic effort to muscle his way through the deadly maelstrom beneath the falls. As the seconds ticked away in his head he prayed he was getting closer to the surface and not just swimming in circles, wasting valuable time.

The pain in his chest deepened as the air that filled his lungs was gradually depleted. And, as much as he wanted to take another breath, he had to force his mouth shut to prevent what little air remained from escaping too soon and admitting a flood of water. However, through a cloud of despair came a glimmer of hope when some renegade air bubbles squeezed between his pursed lips. He felt the bubbles tickle his nose. Then he watched them drift upward and vanish in a blur of water. Finally he knew which way he had to go to break through the murkiness that covered him like a death robe.

With his lungs about to burst, he fought his way to the surface. However, before he emerged his insides exploded and his first gulp of air was tainted by the sea. He floundered at the surface, hacking and coughing, desperately trying to purge his lungs of the briny liquid. Only the water kept coming and before long he was slipping beneath the buffeting waves once again, sinking deeper and deeper, into the yawning blackness.

He felt something brush against him. Then jab at his shoulder and neck as if searching for a tender place to sink its teeth into. He reached across to sweep the thing away, expecting his hand to be devoured, torn to shreds by a mouthful of vicious, razor sharp teeth. However, instead of feeling the might of its bite, his knuckles stung from knocking on something much more solid than flesh and bones.

As he slipped in and out of consciousness he could feel the object tapping his hand, imploring him to grab on to the hooked end; but his mind was drifting, floating. He was past the point of caring when the object lashed out and delivered a crushing blow that hurt so much his head briefly cleared; long enough for him to realize the desperation of the situation. He forced his hand through the curve and held fast. He sensed he was being dragged upwards but lost consciousness long before reaching the surface.

●　　　●　　　●　　　●

While Kyle was blacking out for want of oxygen, Megan and Lumpy were up to their necks in water and, as grim as things looked for the hapless pair, they were in no immediate danger thanks to a bond of fear that brought them together the moment Kyle went after Jan and left them standing in the dark. As much as Megan loathed rubbing shoulders with Lumpy, she hated the gloomy underground grotto even more. And so it was that she found herself wedged between a shallow recess in the cavern wall and the last person in the world she would have wanted to hold hands with. Luckily, there was no one around to witness her humiliation.

For his part, Lumpy had no idea how long he had been standing in the chilly water with his back pressed against the cavern wall, but he knew if he let Megan hold onto his hand much longer her claw-like fingers were going to pierce the skin. He felt the talons digging into his flesh and said behind gritted teeth, "You can let go now. The water seems to have leveled off and I really don't think we're going anywhere."

Megan was reluctant to release her grip for fear that as soon as she let go Lumpy was going to sneak away, leaving her behind to fend for herself. Of course, if he really wanted to be nasty, he could always push her in the raging torrent and be rid of her once and for all.

"I can't," said Megan, squeezing his hand harder and digging her claws deeper.

"Ouch!" Lumpy pulled his hand away suddenly, wincing in pain.

Megan felt a twinge in her left shoulder.

"Do you always have to be so rough?" she said, massaging her aching shoulder.

"Do you always have to be so stupid?"

Lumpy held his throbbing hand out of the water and ran the fingers of his other hand over the claw marks. The skin was wet to the touch, although, there was nothing to suggest the dampness was anything other than water. He lowered his hands. Then he moved away from Megan, using his back to feel his way along the cavern wall.

"Hey! What are doing?" shrieked Megan.

"What do you think I'm doing? I'm going to look for Kyle and Jan."

"Not without me you're not."

Megan reached out in the dark, brushing the air with her hand until she was able to latch onto Lumpy's shirt. She didn't expect him to offer her his hand again, so she held on tightly to the sleeve, shuffling sideways to keep up.

●   ●   ●   ●

Kyle woke with a start, coughing so hard it felt like someone had just detonated a bomb inside his head. His ears were still ringing when he rolled onto his side and coughed up what looked like a small lake and the undigested contents of his stomach. Through the hacking and coughing that followed he saw a shadow appear beside him. It was Jan. He could tell by the shape of the shadow and the familiar sound of her voice.

"You did it," said Jan joyfully. "I thought for sure he was dead but you kept telling me otherwise."

"He wasn't under long enough," said a nervous voice. "He merely lost consciousness and quickly recovered once I helped him get rid of all that water he swallowed."

As Kyle listened to the stranger he vaguely recalled a weight bearing down on him, pressing against his rib cage and pumping his lungs to expel the salty water. He felt a pang in his chest and knew how the stranger had brought him back from the dead. Under the circumstances he welcomed the pain and looked forward to meeting the person who had saved his life. But not before he made himself more presentable. He slipped a hand under his shirt and pressed the sodden cloth to his face, soaking up the chunks of vomit around his mouth and dangling from his nose on a thread. Then he rolled onto his back.

The first thing he saw was Jan's bright face, hovering over him like a beacon. Long, golden locks, which took on a rusty tinge in the orange tinted sky, hung limply on either side of an animated smile and pelted him with water.

"Stand back before you really do drown him."

Jan giggled in embarrassment.

"Sorry!"

As Jan stepped back, Kyle caught sight of a scrawny, ragged figure draped in threadbare sackcloth and holding a long, wooden staff, hooked at one end. Dark smudges encircled large bulging eyes, which tended to dart here and there rather than look directly at you. Kyle was too busy gawking at the oversized, pointed ears to take notice of the wandering eyes.

"Before you ask, yes, they're real and, no, you can't pull on them to make sure," said the stranger.

He threw Jan a stern look.

Kyle opened his mouth to say something but nothing came out. Jan was eager to speak so she jumped in at the first opportunity.

"His name is Ewewyrd and he's an elf."

"Lesser elf," corrected Ewewyrd. "An unfortunate result of interbreeding, a practice that is no longer tolerated, between the light elves of Alfheim and the dark elves of Darkalfheim."

He glanced around nervously before extending a hairy hand.

The stranger was shorter than Jan so all Kyle had to do was reach up to take the proffered hand.

"Kyle Dunlop. I suppose I should thank you for saving my life but somehow I get the feeling this is nothing more than a dream."

Kyle sat upright, sinking his hands into the spongy, moss-like blanket he had been lying on. He pulled out a clump of the feathery ground cover and rolled it about with his thumb, marveling at the soft, downy texture.

"Does it feel like a dream?" asked Ewewyrd.

"Not like any I can remember," said Kyle, discarding the clump of moss and rising to his feet.

It felt strange after looking up to Ewewyrd to now have to look down. But even if Kyle stood in his bare feet like Ewewyrd, he was still at least two feet taller than the elf. He could see by the balding head that Ewewyrd was much older than he initially thought.

He looked beyond the balding head at the waterfall and the barely visible opening through which he and Jan had emerged. It was hard to believe they were both still alive and in one piece after being swept away by the tidal surge and tossed about like rag dolls. Sure, Jan had the life jacket, which probably saved her from drowning and cushioned her from any crushing blows. But nothing short of a miracle could have saved them from surviving that drop. As Kyle followed the water's descent he estimated the plunge in his head, and while he would never be able to prove it, he was convinced the waterfall was over two hundred feet high. Just thinking about it made his head spin.

Jan spoke in a tentative voice, breaking Kyle's train of thought and sparing him any further cranial discomfort. "I do hope nothing terrible has happened to Megan." She shivered and chattered her teeth. "Or Lumpy," she added as an afterthought.

Kyle noticed her trembling and wondered if it was because she was cold or afraid of what he might say. He also saw that the brilliant smile which had warmed his heart earlier had faded, leaving behind a face clouded with worry. She suddenly looked very small and fragile.

"I'm sure they're fine," said Kyle unconvincingly.

Tears welled up in Jan's eyes. Feeling her anguish, Kyle reached out and let Jan fall into his arms and bury her face in his chest. He wrapped his arms around her, holding her close for comfort.

At the mention of Megan and Lumpy, Ewewyrd's eyeballs nearly popped out of their sockets. His eyes darted back and forth at a dizzying pace.

"Do you mean to say there are others just like you up there?" He glanced at the hole atop the waterfall, pausing to see if anyone else was going to pop out. When no one else appeared, he added. "King Bruide is not going to like this. He's not going to like this at all."

"King Bruide?" chorused Kyle and Jan.

Kyle loosened his grip and stepped away from Jan, allowing himself an unobstructed view of his surroundings. And what he saw through the orangey glow confounded and amazed him. This wasn't just another vast cavern buried deep inside the bowels of the earth and inhabited by strange people, like Ewewyrd. It was a secret subterranean world—a part of the planet earth that no one knew existed—bathed in shimmering, orange light and teeming with life. While sheep grazed lazily on the near side of a river that cut a wide swath in the land, row after row of carefully tended plots lined the opposite bank. The plots stretched upward and outward for as far as the eye could see, flowing along a broad bend in the river and giving away briefly to a stone bridge that spanned the waterway. A beaten earth path crossed the bridge and followed the gentle slope up to the gates of a guarded community secreted away behind a formidable stone wall.

Kyle noticed a figure stirring on one of the crenellated guard towers that ringed the octagonal wall. A moment later a warning horn boomed out over the roar of the waterfall.

"Oh, no!" uttered Ewewyrd, visibly distressed.

"What's wrong?" wondered Kyle.

Ewewyrd paced back and forth, tugging on his hair.

"Everything," he said.

No sooner had Ewewyrd made this announcement than the gates groaned open and parted with a creak. As soon as the gap was wide enough three horsemen, the lead rider astride a powerful black charger and the other two straddling much smaller brown nags, stormed through the opening.

Ewewyrd saw the horsemen coming their way and became more agitated.

"What to do? What to do?" he muttered, yanking harder on his hair and stomping about like a nervous hen.

Kyle decided to stop him before he pulled out what little hair remained on his head.

"Why are you so afraid? Surely those men don't mean to harm us?"

"Who's to say wwwhat they'll do?" stammered Ewewyrd. "They're the kings men and the king doesn't take kindly to strangers—" He paused to catch his breath and chomp on his nails when a frail figure hunched with age had to leap aside to avoid being trampled by the charging horses. "—or anyone caught associating with them."

"But we haven't done anything wrong," said Jan bemused.

Ewewyrd shrugged his shoulders.

"It doesn't matter. The king thinks all outsiders are spies or thieves, until they are able to prove otherwise."

Jan was puzzled by this last remark and was about to ask Ewewyrd why on earth the king would believe such a thing but she didn't have time. Once the elf saw the riders cross the bridge and head towards them, he clucked like a scared chicken and ducked behind Kyle.

"You never saw me. You never saw me," he babbled, over and over, fainter and fainter, until the words were drowned out by the waterfall.

The leader pulled back on the reins to check his horse within a few feet of Kyle and Jan. The beast stopped abruptly, rearing and snuffling as its forelegs came down hard and tore into the spongy ground. Meanwhile, one of his henchmen rode onwards to scour the riverbank, while the other one circled the intruders.

Whatever the second henchman was searching for he didn't find, but it wasn't hard to guess. Somehow Ewewyrd had managed to vanish into thin air and, as much as the leader of the welcoming committee tried to hide his disappointment when his henchman approached him with a confused look on his face, he failed.

"Who are you? And what are you doing here?" the leader growled, fixing Kyle and Jan with a suspicious glower.

His name was Loki and he was a short, powerfully built goblin with a barrel chest, well-muscled arms and thighs, and a toadlike face full of warts. Someone should have told him before he got on his charger that the dark grey doublet he sported was much too small for his large frame because he kept tugging at the collar, as if it was choking him. Perhaps this was the reason for his tetchiness.

"Well!" Loki snapped when no one volunteered to answer. "Are you going to talk or shall I tell Jorge here to knock some sense into you?"

Jorge was more massive than Loki. However, much of the extra bulk was fat; his sleeveless tunic exposing two flabby arms the size of melons. He was also rather witless. A fact that wasn't lost on Kyle and Jan as the dimwit gazed at them through vacant eyes, pounding a blood-stained cudgel suggestively in his massive hand.

Jan wanted to turn away but she found that she couldn't. There was something about the grotesque figure grinning stupidly behind a mouthful of rotten, pitted teeth that reminded her of Lumpy. She tried to picture the two together, wearing the same clothes and, if not for the warts and multiple chins, Jorge could have easily passed for Lumpy's older brother. She almost burst out laughing. Then the idiot started snickering and drool began to dribble out of his mouth and run down his chin. Her lip curled in disgust.

Loki sensed Jan's discomfort and assaulted her with an ill-humored grin. "I'd hate to see what you'd look like after Jorge gets through with you."

Jan shot back.

"I doubt I would look any uglier than you, toad-face."

She thrust out her jaw.

Loki drew his sword and pointed it threateningly at Jan.

"Mind your tongue, little one, or I'll cut it out!"

Jan poked out her tongue and dared him to try. Kyle groaned inwardly.

Fortunately the other member of the welcoming committee, a mirror image of Loki but wearing a sleeveless tunic just like Jorge, had just returned from combing the riverbank. Loki was so distracted by what the fellow was holding in his right hand that he forgot all about the insolent pipsqueak standing before him breathing defiance.

"What in Thor's name is that?" said Loki.

"I'm not sure, captain," the fellow said in a raspy voice, "but it looks like some sort of weapon." A clever smile creased his warty face. "They must have pitched it in the river when they saw us coming down the hill."

He puffed out his chest and stared accusingly at Kyle and Jan. His eyes were as sharp and cruel as any hawks.

Loki must have jumped to the same conclusion. "Good man, Rydd! I knew these two were up to no good."

"Weapon!" blurted Kyle. "Are you crazy? That isn't a weapon. It's a flashlight. And if you'll allow me, I'll show you three simpletons how it works."

Kyle stepped forward but Loki promptly stayed him with the sword.

"Take another step and I'll run you through."

Kyle could see that Loki was dead serious so he stood his ground.

Rydd observed his find through new eyes. He rolled the flashlight back and forth several times, feeling around with his stubby fingers for anything that might give him a clue as to how it worked. Much to his chagrin, he realized too late that he should not have pressed down on the small bump near the shiny end of the device. The pressure switch beneath his thumb made a sharp 'click', sending forth a beam of light that hit Loki square in the face.

Loki dropped his sword and squealed like a pig, throwing his arms up to shield his eyes from the brilliant light. Somehow he managed to dig in his spurs and the charger lunged forward unexpectedly. Only some quick thinking and incredible horsemanship kept him from being thrown from the saddle. As he struggled to calm the startled beast, Rydd turned off the flashlight. Meanwhile, Jorge jumped down to retrieve the sword before Kyle or Jan could pounce on it.

Jan was too busy laughing her head off to even notice the sword and, for a moment, Kyle thought he heard someone else giggling, as well. He knew it couldn't be Rydd or Jorge, so that left only one other person; Ewewyrd. Somehow, the elf had managed to vanish into thin air, leaving him and Jan to deal with Loki and his henchmen. He wanted to know how he could make himself invisible too and thought of whispering to see if he could get Ewewyrd's attention, but he knew that wouldn't be wise.

Loki was fuming. "So you think that's funny, do you?"

He edged the charger closer to Jan. Then he leaned down, baring his teeth and piercing her with his cold dark eyes.

"You won't be laughing when I get through with you."

Jan edged closer to Kyle for protection.

Loki noticed the fear in Jan's eyes and, as he sat straight in the saddle again, a satisfied smirk animated his ugly face.

"Tie them up!" he roared.

Rydd was about to dismount and assist Jorge, who had already gathered some rope, when Loki barked at him.

"Wait!"

Rydd paused, leaning halfway out of the saddle at on awkward angle.

Loki rode alongside Rydd and held out his hand.

"Give me that thing before you blind someone."

The flashlight slid from Rydd's into Loki's hand. Then, just as smoothly, Rydd slid out of the saddle and fell with a thud to the ground.

Jan's lips quivered and turned upwards slightly, but somehow she swallowed the laugh stuck in her throat.

Loki gave her a dark scowl.

"We'll soon find out what you're really doing in Midgard."

•　　　•　　　•　　　•

Megan could feel the water swirling around her, tugging on her chest, her back, her aching legs; desperately trying to draw her away from the relative security of the cavern wall. She could also feel herself growing tired, losing strength, barely able to cling to the wall and the one life-line, the one thing that was really keeping her from being carried away; Lumpy's filthy shirt. She wanted to beg him to stop and let her rest, but she knew he wouldn't listen. He was determined to find Kyle and Jan, and no amount of begging was going to slow him down.

There was a new sense of urgency in Lumpy's step as they rounded a projection in the cavern wall and, as the tension on Megan's arm grew, she knew she wouldn't be able to hold on to him much longer. But little did she know that the sudden change of pace was more by accident than by design. Even Lumpy's great bulk was no match for the faster water surging through the narrow channel on the other side of the rocky outcrop. She felt him being sucked into the channel and, by the time they both realized what was happening, it was too late. Once he was swept off his feet, she had no choice but to follow.

4
FAIRY DUST

ON A KNOLL, in the heart of Midgard, stood the royal palace; a sprawling, two-story, stonework building surrounded by a protective curtain wall and topped by four gilt tiled towers that provided an unobstructed view of the bustling city below. From the central portcullised gateway a paved walkway, lined with golden statues dedicated to the memory of goblin monarchs and heroes, led to a wide, white marble staircase. Atop the steps was an elaborate arched entrance and emblazoned above it, for everyone to see, was a central gold ring surrounded by eight identical, interlocking gold rings.

Less inviting than the entrance was the dungeon, a cold, dark space consisting of no more than a handful of cramped cells hewn from solid rock and lining either side of a natural fissure. Dirty and dank, depressing and gloomy, it was the last place in the world anyone would want to be if given the option. A sliver of light peeking through a crack between the rough stone floor and a sturdy wooden door meant that one of the cells was occupied; but obviously not by choice.

Inside, a tallow candle burned with an ethereal glow, casting monstrous shadows in the tiny cell. An unusually plump spider hanging from a thread was caught in the flickering light and projected against one of the walls. Its reflection grew to hideously large proportions then returned to normal, as the curiosity that had lured the arachnid towards the candle was suppressed by the intense heat. Reeling from the flame, the spider quickly descended and disappeared behind a restless figure lying curled up on the hard stone floor.

For the longest time Kyle stood and watched as Jan drifted in and out of sleep; a fitful sleep occasioned by violent bouts of sneezing and incessant shivering. He would have dearly liked to comfort her but, with only the shirt on his back to offer his little sister, and a wet shirt at that, there was little he could do. At least she had the sense to listen to him when he suggested she use the orange life jacket to prop her head off the floor. It was better than nothing he reasoned and, while it pained her to agree with him, it was more useful as a pillow than as a blanket. In time her body stopped shaking and her breathing grew shallower and he knew she would not stir again for quite some time.

Kyle had been so busy worrying about Jan that he didn't realize until it was almost too late just how exhausted he was. With his legs ready to collapse underneath him he leaned against the wall and slid to the ground, grimacing as his aching left shoulder scraped against the rough surface.

Tears filled his eyes, but he wasn't sure if they came as a result of the pain he was experiencing or the mental anguish weighing heavily on his mind. If only he hadn't been so selfish, Megan and Lumpy would be safe and Jan wouldn't be lying here shivering. The thought of all the grief he had caused was too much to bear. He closed his eyes and tried to battle the despair that threatened to engulf him.

By the time Kyle opened his eyes again the candle, which had been three fingers high the last time he looked, had burned down to nothing. All that remained was a puddle of melted wax and a flickering yellow flame encircling a blackened wick. The flame sputtered and hissed, dancing around the sea of wax. Dreading the moment the flame expired, Kyle gazed at the fiery image with the hope of holding onto the light long after the cell went pitch-black.

The sound of shuffling feet and muffled voices beyond the confines of the cell drew his attention away from the flame. Eager to catch a few snippets of what was being said he cautiously slid closer to the door and pressed his ear to a crack along the outer edge. Unfortunately, the scuffing and murmuring ceased abruptly and he thought for sure that whoever had been wandering around outside was gone. Then he sensed a presence on the other side of the door and, a moment later, someone began playing with the latch. He jumped back as the door of the cell swung open.

"Kyle...Jan?" came a familiar voice.

Kyle leapt to his feet.

"Ewewyrd?" he said in astonishment. He peered at the opening but all he could see was the dimly lit corridor. "Where are you?"

"Over here."

Kyle glanced around in vain.

"Where? I can't see you."

Someone much bigger than Ewewyrd could possibly be threw an arm around his neck, gripping him in a headlock and blowing stale breath on his cheek.

"Of course you can't. He's invisible and so am I."

"Lumpy!" Kyle croaked. He pushed at the air, stumbling backwards as he broke free. "I thought I'd never see you again."

"You still can't," said Lumpy. "Thanks to Ewewyrd's magical fairy dust."

Unseen, Lumpy rumpled Kyle's hair.

"Cut it out," said Kyle, swiping at the air.

He pinned his back against the wall of the cell and extended his arms, bracing himself for another attack; but it didn't come.

"Where's Megan?" said Kyle relaxing slightly, his voice ringing with concern.

"Don't worry," giggled Jan. "She's over here with me".

Just before the flame fizzled and went out, Kyle caught a glimpse of Jan sitting up and hugging the air. While he was relieved to see that she had sprung to life and some of the natural color had returned to her cheeks, he was more relieved to hear that everyone had managed to make it through the cave safely. All they had to do now was make good their escape and find a way out of this strange, subterranean world. It seemed so simple once he learned more about Ewewyrd's magical fairy dust.

Kyle felt a tingling sensation course through his veins and attributed it to the glittery gold fairy dust Ewewyrd had just sprinkled over him.

"Why didn't you tell me about this stuff when you saw those three goons coming towards us?" said Kyle. "We probably wouldn't be here now, if you did."

He watched his hands and arms disappear, followed by the rest of his body.

"I would have," Ewewyrd assured him, "but not only does the fairy dust wear off naturally, it dissolves instantly in water. And, at the time, you were both soaking wet."

"That's why we took so long to get here," said Megan. "After Ewewyrd fished us out of the water he took us back to his hut and, as much as we wanted to come for you right away, we had to sit around and wait until our clothes had dried completely. It wasn't easy but, so far, Ewewyrd's plan has worked to perfection."

"Save the chatter for later," grumbled Lumpy. "I want to get out of this place before I start sweating like a pig and blow my cover."

Lumpy wasn't the only one itching to get going. Ewewyrd, through no fault of his own, was in this up to his ears and, if Loki or one of his goons ever got their hands on him, they would lock him up, probably inside this very same cell, and throw away the key. With visions of the last time he ran afoul of the law he reached inside a tattered sheepskin pouch and removed a handful of fairy dust. Then he showered Jan with golden flakes.

The fairy dust was promptly soaked up by Jan's hair, her arms, her clothes, and every other part of her anatomy it came in contact with. As she began to vanish before Ewewyrd's eyes, he secured the pouch with a drawstring and placed it for safe keeping in a secret pocket inside his sackcloth tunic.

And not a moment too soon as heavy footsteps could be heard descending the staircase that led to the dungeon.

"Take my hand," Ewewyrd whispered in Jan's ear.

Jan probed the darkness and touched something hairy. With images of spiders fresh in her mind she gasped and withdrew her hand.

But Ewewyrd was too quick. He grabbed Jan's wrist and held tightly. Then he and Jan located the others and led them by the hand out of the cell.

No sooner had they vacated the cell when Rydd rounded a corner and appeared at the foot of the stairs. He stopped dead in his tracks and gaped at the open door.

Jorge was so focused on what he was doing, keeping a watchful eye on the food tray he was carrying, that he failed to notice that Rydd had halted on the bottom step. Needless to say, he slammed into his colleague, upsetting the tray and dumping the contents of two bowls of gruel on the unfortunate goblin's head. The mushy, pasty liquid flowed like hot lava over Rydd's greasy hair, plopping onto his rounded shoulders and running down the nape of his neck. In the meantime, the near empty bowls hit the stone floor and shattered into countless pieces.

"Fool!" shouted Rydd. "Why don't you watch where you're going?"

"You told me to keep my eyes on the tray. You never said anything about watching where I was going."

Jorge's eyes went to the tray that he held within inches of Rydd's runny nose.

"Quiet!"

Rydd batted the tray away, waves of steam rising up from the clods of hot gruel still clinging to his hair. "We don't have time for this nonsense. We have to find those two before they get us into more trouble than we are already in, you fool."

"The king's not going to like this. Is he Rydd?"

"I don't give a fig what the king likes or doesn't like!" said Rydd behind a troubled look. "It's Loki I aim to please and, if he ever finds out we let those two escape it'll be troll duty for you and me."

Jorge blanched. "Troll duty!" he gasped.

"Troll duty," echoed Rydd. "And you know what happens if you get too close to a troll."

Rydd eyed a clump of gruel on the floor, making sure Jorge was regarding it too before he lifted one stubby leg high in the air and stomped down, grinding the remnants of the mushy lump into the hard stone floor.

Jorge moaned, twisting his ugly features into a pained expression.

Jan didn't know what turned her stomach more, Jorge's hideous mug or the putrid smelling gruel. Did they actually think she was going to eat that stuff? She held her breath and flattened herself against the wall when Rydd came to within inches of her and paused. He was looking directly at her with a baffled expression on his face.

For a moment Jan thought he was going to reach out and take her by the throat, so she turned her head away and prepared herself for the worst. But instead of placing his cold, icy hands around her neck, he caressed her cheek with his stale, fetid breath when he reached up to remove a flaming torch from the wall bracket just above her head. As he backed away, she exhaled and shivered, sending waves of fear throughout the chain of bodies linked hand in hand against the wall.

Rydd strode over and peered inside the cell. It didn't take a genius to see that it was empty. He cursed his luck.

"They've got to be around here somewhere," he growled. He eyed the stairs. "There's only one way out of here and I didn't see anyone come up those stairs. Did you?"

Jorge stared blankly at the stairs. Then he shook his head from side to side, spraying the torch with spittle and making the flame splutter.

"Well then. What are we waiting for?" said Rydd shortly. "Take this and go through those cells over there." He waved the torch at a block of cells to his right then he handed it to Jorge. "I'll go get another torch and look through these cells here." This time he fluttered his hand at a similar block of cells to his left. He raised his voice and added. "One way or another we'll flush them out. And when we do—"

Without warning, Rydd slammed the door of the vacant cell shut. The resulting echo sounded like a cannon.

Jan and the others had started to creep towards the stairs when they were startled by the loud boom. They jumped in the air and came back down to earth as one, but otherwise reacted as individuals. While Kyle clamped a hand over his mouth and Lumpy held his breath, Megan shrieked and Jan let out of shrill scream. Ewewyrd simply piddled in his pants.

Rydd spun round to face the stairs. At first he was confused by what he saw, or rather, didn't see. Then he noticed the puddle and saw two feet, two elfish feet, materializing out of thin air.

"You!" he hollered. "I should have known you had something to do with this. You won't get away from us this time, Ewewyrd."

At the sound of his name Ewewyrd broke away from the others and bolted for the stairs. The two disembodied feet plopped through the mess on the floor, leaving a telltale trail on the stone steps.

One footprint after another was cast in gruel until Rydd counted a total of four more pairs of feet dashing for the stairs. The sound of thumping feet and panic-stricken voices filled the stairwell. It would have been a scene of utter chaos if the five terrified figures scrabbling up the winding staircase were the least bit visible.

"Follow those feet!" said Rydd in a loud, booming voice.

Jorge handed Rydd the torch and lumbered towards the staircase. Rydd gazed in astonishment at the flickering flame before tossing aside the torch and charging up the stairs after everyone.

The plan was simple. Stick together, no matter what, and follow Ewewyrd's lead. That way they would all get out of the palace safely. Nothing more. Nothing less. It wasn't worth thinking about what would happen if they got separated because the elf was the only one who knew his way around and, without him, they were lost. But the unthinkable had happened and no one, except Ewewyrd, had a clue where they were supposed to be going.

"Head for the far exit!" screamed Ewewyrd, as he reached the top of the stairs and barged into the unoccupied guard room above the dreary dungeon.

On passing by a doorway to his right, Ewewyrd glanced back to see if the others were following. Of course, he couldn't see anything because everyone was invisible, but he thought he heard someone breathing heavily not too far behind him. Taking that as a good sign, he turned back and headed straight for the doorway on the far side of the room. It may not have been the shortest route to take but he knew from experience it was the surest. At least, it should have been, if only Loki hadn't appeared out of nowhere and gotten in the way.

Ewewyrd tried to stop short but whoever was trailing ploughed into him from behind. Catapulted forward, he crashed into Loki, bouncing off the goblin's paunch and knocking Jan, who was following close on his heels, to the ground. Loki spotted the elf's hairy feet doing a jig and heard Jan scream, and seized the pair before they had time to recover and escape.

"What's this?" said Loki. "Fairy dust? I would have thought you learned your lesson, elf."

He spat out the last word, almost as if it left behind a bad taste in his mouth.

From all the hacking and squawking going on it was obvious that Loki had Ewewyrd by the throat and that Jan's jaw was left free to flap.

"Let him go, toad face! Can't you see you're choking him? Ouch! You're hurting me, you brute."

"Shut your mouth or I'll wring your neck, too. Ah..."

Shocked, Loki's left arm flew upward and his fist jerked open. He gazed at his aching hand, long enough to notice the marks where Jan's teeth had sank in. Then he sliced through the air and clenched his fist around what felt like her scrawny neck.

"Have it your way," said Loki.

A strangled squeal brought a satisfied grin to the goblin's face.

The smile faded as Loki was distracted by a commotion on the other side of the room. He watched with interest as first Jorge then Rydd came into view. Jorge was hunched over with his back to Loki, while Rydd was further away facing him. Somewhere, between the two, was an adversary of considerable size, if the pained expression on Rydd's mottled face was any indication.

As they approached the top of the stairwell it looked like the goblins had things under control until Rydd, who was panting and sweating profusely, lost his hold for a moment and fell backwards. Luckily, the wall broke his fall or he would have surely tumbled down the stairs, along with Jorge and the person they were grappling with. He bounced back and took a better grip.

In response to being yanked forward and thrown off balance, Jorge heaved back with all his might and, as he did so, he caught his heel on the top step. Since there was nothing to stop him from falling, he stumbled backwards into the chamber and hit the floor with a thud, his thick arms still looped around open air.

Rydd flew through the air and crashed down next to Jorge, who seemed to be rolling around all by himself.

"Hold onto him, Jorge!" Rydd shouted, as he made a beeline for some rope lying on the floor next to a table and chair. There was a bucket and two wooden cups on the table.

When Rydd scurried back he saw Jorge thrashing about on the floor. He dropped to his knees and grabbed at the air. Once. Twice. Finally, he caught hold of what felt like a shin bone. He tugged on the leg, helping Jorge roll his opponent, who had very little fight left in him, onto his back.

Jorge promptly pounced on his opponent's stomach, knocking the wind out of the fellow and giving Rydd just enough time to locate the other leg and gather it in. It took some time but eventually Rydd was able to fasten the rope around both arms and legs.

While Rydd was busy binding Lumpy's limbs, Kyle and Megan were tripping about in the dark, searching for an exit that didn't exist. In spite of Ewewyrd's warning, it seemed like such a good idea at the time to turn right at the top of the stairs and duck into an adjacent chamber, avoiding Loki altogether. But now that they had time to think about it, they knew they had made a mistake; a grave mistake. They were trapped like rats. And it was only a matter of time before someone thought to look for them in this dead end of a room. They decided to arm themselves. So, while Kyle stumbled across a metal poker, Megan put her hands on a tall glass cylinder that felt like it would make a good club.

They didn't have long to wait. They heard Jan scream, along with the sound of water being dumped and splashing on the floor. A moment later the doorway was illuminated and Loki's intimidating frame stood silhouetted in the opening. He carried a torch in one hand and, in the other hand, he held Jan by the scruff of the neck. Jan was grim faced and dripping wet.

Megan shrieked and swooned, sending the glass container she

was clutching close to her body crashing to the floor with her. Her disembodied head seemed to suddenly appear out of nowhere, resting in a pool of clear, viscous liquid. It was surrounded by a dozen or more eyeballs and shards of broken glass.

Kyle's heart leapt to his throat as he gazed around and saw the room for what it was; a torture chamber full unspeakable horrors. Leg irons and heavy collared chains dangled from the walls. A charred, bird-like cage secured by a rope and pulley that was bracketed to the ceiling and fastened to a nearby wall hung over a charcoal brazier. A rack, for pulling the limbs in different directions until tendons tore or bones cracked, stood in the centre of the room. The most gruesome discovery was on a table next to where Megan lay unconscious: jars of eyeballs, ears and other assorted organs suspended in a clear, viscous solution. A pair of iron tongs on the table was stained red with blood. Had Kyle not been so worried about Jan, he, too, may have passed out.

Loki had his eyes fixed on the iron rod floating in midair. "You can make this easy on yourself, or—" He tightened his grip on Jan's neck.

Jan gasped for air as she yanked on Loki's fingers, but she couldn't make them budge. Even when she scratched at them and drew blood they held firmly.

The iron rod hit the floor with a clank.

"I knew you would see things my way," Loki said with a grim smile.

He relaxed his grip, allowing the color to return to Jan's face.

"Now, if you don't mind, the king is waiting. Afterwards, we'll come back here and I'll show you how everything works."

He glowed proudly in the torchlight.

Kyle observed the dark expression on the goblin's face and the thought of returning to Loki's *chamber of horrors* made him feel sick to his stomach.

5
THE GOBLIN KING

LOKI LED KYLE and the others through a maze of dimly lit passages and up a flight of steps. Along the way the somber procession passed by the kitchen, sparking an incident that left the scullions and cooks, a collection of jittery, malnourished elves, similar in many respects to Ewewyrd, visibly shaken. Like a magnet Lumpy was drawn in by the kitchen's tempting smells, much to the dismay of the terrified elves who took one look at the madman who had invaded their domain and fled, bleating like a flock of sheep beset by wolves. It took Rydd and Jorge several minutes to extricate Lumpy from the scene, but not before he had managed to lay his hands on almost everything in sight. He was still licking his fingers clean when they reached the top of the stairs.

They came upon a sea of marble, skillfully arranged in workable sized tiles and highly polished to reflect the modest light. Rising up from the white marble floor were two rows of gilt-trimmed, green marble columns that spanned the entire length of the foyer, from a spectacular arched entrance at one end to the sturdy wooden doors of the great hall at the other end. The hardwood panels were flanked by two burly, pike-wielding guards who seemed to spawn to life from the images of a mighty battle scene carved into the ancient woodwork.

Loki guided his charges across the foyer and around the columns, marching them to within a few paces of the double doors of the great hall. He ordered Kyle and Jan, then Megan and Lumpy to form two lines facing the doors. They were backed up by Rydd and Jorge. The only sign of acknowledgement by either guard was a fleeting look of disdain on one face, accompanied by a more protracted scowl on the other.

Kyle wasn't sure if the dark looks were directed at him and his companions, or Loki and his two henchmen. He had a better idea who the guards loathed more once Loki strode past the pair, growling at them in a surly manner as he let himself into the great hall. The senior guard regarded Loki's retreating back with undisguised menace, probably wishing he could run his pike, held with a white-knuckled grip, through Loki's thick skull. Instead, he slammed the door, which Loki had left wide open, closed again.

With the source of the irritation gone, both guards focused their attention elsewhere, furrowing their brows in an attempt to make sense of the four oddities facing them. Perhaps if they had listened more closely to the teachings of the ancient ones, they would have realized the strangers were human beings; a fiercely proud and rebellious race of lesser mortals. As it was, they barely had time to satisfy their curiosity before the doors of the great hall flew open and Loki reappeared.

Loki rushed forward and the two guards opened the doors wider.

Curious to catch a glimpse of the great hall, Jan tried to peer around Loki but he made a point of halting directly in front of her, deliberately blocking her view. Once again she found herself gagging on his stale, fetid breath. She wondered if he was married and, if he was, she felt sorry for the poor goblin woman who had to wake up every morning and catch a whiff of such an unsavory odor.

"Listen up!" he snarled. "There are four things to remember before you enter."

He held up a fist and started the count by flicking his index finger in Jan's face. "Keep your mouth shut unless you are invited to speak." The second finger flipped up and brushed her nose. "If you do get a chance to say something, make it brief." Another finger came into view. "And never—ever—question the king." Finally the pinkie appeared. "Should you fail to heed my advice—" He pierced Jan with his dark, dagger-like eyes. "—I'll rip out your *tongue!*"

With an intimidating flick of the wrist his open hand was transformed back into a fist.

Jan was so startled that she stepped back, stomping on Lumpy's foot. He grimaced in pain.

Loki flashed a triumphant smile.

"Follow me!" he said, before turning on his heels and advancing towards the hall.

Kyle and Jan moved forward reluctantly. Megan and Lumpy didn't budge until they were prodded from behind by Rydd and Jorge.

The great hall was even more spectacular than the marble foyer. Not only because it was illuminated by a gigantic candle wheel suspended from the ceiling, but the rough stone walls found throughout much of the palace were cleverly disguised by elaborately woven tapestries that spoke of a past steeped in myth and legend. A time when giants, trolls and other fearsome creatures roamed all levels of the planet earth and the 'little people' fought alongside the gods. Even the marble floor was softened by a strip of plush red carpet that ran down the center of the room, from just beyond the entrance to a golden throne at the other end.

The throne was standing on a platform draped in crimson velvet. And sitting on the throne was a big, fleshy goblin wearing a richly jeweled crown and a purple, fur-lined robe made of the finest silk and embroidered with the royal insignia; a central golden ring surrounded by eight identical, interlocking gold rings.

Over the years, idleness and excess had added a degree of puffiness to the king's features, not to mention the addition of several chins, making him appear soft and weak. But you had to look no further than his keen, watchful eyes to see that this was an illusion. Fair but firm, he was capable of ruling with an iron fist, as anyone who ever aggravated him knew.

To the king's left a withered, melancholic attendant languidly gripped what appeared to be the royal scepter. A long twisted rod tapered downward to a point and surmounted by a dimpled ruby crystal the size of a child's fist. On the other side of the king stood a second attendant; a grotesque figure, nearly as wide as he was tall, with rolls of fat plowing deep furrows in his skin-tight tunic. In one of his ham-handed fists he clutched the flashlight that Rydd had fished out of the river.

Loki ordered Kyle and the others to stop when they were several paces from the dais. Then he stepped aside to allow King Bruide an unobstructed view of the detainees.

The king's gaze ran over each of them, weighing, appraising.

"You," he said, regarding Kyle suspiciously. "Who sent you and why?"

He possessed a deep-throated, rumbling voice that spoke of power and authority. Kyle noticed the scowl lines etched deeply on his stern face and his first thought was that this was not someone to cross.

"No one sent us, your Highness, sir. We—er—dropped in by accident."

The king pounced on the slight pause.

"Liar! Do you take me for a fool? No one comes here without a purpose. And what yours is I can only imagine."

He frowned severely at Kyle.

"You can imagine what you like," said Megan bristling. "We arrived by accident just as Kyle said and the sooner we can leave here, the better."

She crossed her arms in defiance and returned the king's angry look.

"Guard your tongue!" Loki hissed, unsheathing his sword and moving menacingly towards Megan.

The king stayed Loki with an imperial wave of his hand.

"Wait! Perhaps you should refrain from punishing the wench until after they've been put to the test. I would hate to see her suffer unfairly."

The smoke from a dying candle seemed to swirl like steam around Loki's head as he paused and slid the blade back in the scabbard.

"What of their attempt to escape? And the fairy dust?" Loki pointed out. "Doesn't that prove they are in league with someone?"

"All that proves is they were foolish enough to get mixed up with that troublesome elf," said King Bruide. "It speaks nothing of their innocence or guilt. We'll leave that up to the staff to decide."

The gloomy attendant perked up slightly when he heard the word the staff so he was already prepared to hand over the rod when the king extended his arm. As the king took the scepter from the attendant, he leaned forward on it and rose with a grunt. Then he stepped down from the platform.

Kyle and Jan, Megan and Lumpy stole glances at one another. What madness was this they thought?

"This," the king explained, "is the 'staff of life'. It has the power to discern good from evil, truth from untruth, and can be the difference between life and death. All who touch the staff are bound by its decision. All who bare witness are likewise bound. Do not even think for a moment you can hide behind lies and deception because the crystal knows all, sees all. It was made from the blood of a unicorn, and bits of unicorn horn, shaved from this very staff and ground to a fine powder. The dark elves combined both and forged the crystal with the intention of seeing inside a misguided lover's heart. Need I tell you what became of the poor woman when her secret was revealed?"

Megan didn't like the way King Bruide was looking at her. She glanced away to avoid his deep, penetrating eyes.

Sensing Megan's unease, the king waddled forward and thrust the staff between Kyle and Jan. They leaned away to avoid touching the staff and to let Megan take hold of it, if she dared.

"We shall soon see if your presence here is as accidental as you claim," said King Bruide.

His voice had a mocking ring to it.

Her heart thudding, Megan reached out and gripped the ruby crystal. At first it felt cold and hard and lifeless. But then the strangest thing happened. Not only did it warm up and soften to the touch, but it began to beat to the rhythm of her heart. She felt the blood coursing through her body, passing between the crystal and her fingers and back again. And as much as she wanted to tear her hand away, she couldn't find the strength or the will to do so. It was as if the crystal had become an extension of her being. Another living, pulsing organ she simply could not do without.

She was overcome by a sudden flood of emotions that turned over in her mind's eye like so many pages in a book. From one extreme to another, until the darkness that threatened to envelop her was cast aside forever and she was overwhelmed by the most wonderful, blissful feelings. Every happy memory from the past came back to her in an instant and she couldn't have been more at peace with the world or herself.

King Bruide could see that the staff had searched Megan's soul and she was pure of heart, devoid of evil. But even though she had passed the test he wasn't so sure the others would be as lucky. Anxious to confirm his suspicions, he took hold of the scepter and yanked it out of her hand.

While Megan slowly came out of the trance induced by the staff, Kyle, Lumpy and Jan were given the same test. Although there were moments, in which the darker side of human nature tested the limits of their character, they all managed to suppress the wickedness that lurks within each and every one of us.

"The staff has spoken," said King Bruide, as he took the scepter from Jan. "And because the strangers have shown us that their intentions are honorable, we must put aside any doubts we may have had and treat them as our guests."

He waddled back to the throne, handing the staff to the gloomy attendant before plopping down on the cushioned seat.

Kyle glanced at Loki and noticed that his eyes were as cold as death and filled with hatred. He had no desire to prolong their stay.

"It's nice of you to think of us as your guests your Highness, but we really should be going. If we're not home soon our parents will start to wonder what has happened to us."

The thought of his parents brought only pain and sorrow. Kyle turned away from the king so he couldn't see the hurt in his eyes.

Just then Jan sneezed and Lumpy's stomach growled.

"Nonsense!" the king said brusquely. "You're not going anywhere until you've all had a chance to dine with me. In the meantime, we'll have to do something about those wet clothes."

The king combed the room with his eyes as if expecting to find clean, dry clothes at the ready. Then he saw the flashlight and a fleshy smile lit up his toad-like face. The sternness melted from his voice like a snowflake on warm asphalt.

"But first, I'd like to hear more about that magic torch of yours."

6
THE FEAST

KYLE HAD BEEN cold and damp for so long that he almost forgot what it was like to be warm and dry. But a crackling fire and a change of clothes seemed to refresh his memory and lift his spirits.

"It certainly feels good to get out of those wet clothes and into something dry again," he said with relief.

He extended his arms and wiggled his fingers, admiring the velvety texture of the flowing green robe he had been given to wear and absorbing the heat from a hearth built into the guest room wall. His own clothes lay discarded at his feet, still drying out after being doused with water in Loki's dreaded chamber of horrors.

"I'll feel better when I get some food into my stomach," said Lumpy from the comfort of the only chair in the room.

While Kyle's robe hung loosely on his lanky frame, Lumpy's gown was so tight you could make out every ripple and roll of fat underneath it. Kyle suppressed a grin, knowing full well that his friend was always hungry.

"Me too," said Kyle.

The firewood snapped and some sparks shot in the air, so Kyle had to draw his hands away quickly to avoid setting the robe on fire.

"Let's hope someone comes for us soon," added Kyle. "I don't know about your mom and dad, but my parents must be worried sick."

No sooner had the words left his mouth when there was a knock at the door.

Before they had time to respond, the door swung open and a familiar figure appeared in the doorway. The attendant gazed at them with the same doleful expression he wore throughout the proceedings in the great hall, when he stood to the king's left, safeguarding the 'staff of life'. Despite the gloomy face, Kyle was relieved to see that someone other than Loki was going to accompany them to the feast. At least the attendant didn't regard him with the same loathing and contempt as Loki who, on the king's command, grudgingly escorted Kyle and Lumpy to the guest room so that they could change out of their wet clothes and freshen up before the feast. If a bitter enmity exists Kyle has yet to bear witness.

"The king awaits your presence," said the attendant dully.

"Then let's not keep him waiting," said Lumpy with an expectant glint in his eyes.

For such a big person Lumpy could move remarkably fast. In no time at all, he bounced to his feet, grabbed hold of Kyle's baggy sleeve and hauled him across the room to the corridor outside.

Kyle had no doubt that Lumpy could sniff out the food himself, nevertheless, they both chose to wait for the attendant to close the door and lead the way.

The attendant led them along the corridor in stone-faced silence, following its twists and turns, and passing by one closed door after another until they came to a stairwell illuminated by a solitary wall torch. As they descended the narrow, well-worn stairs the murmur of distant voices filled the air like the winds of a gathering storm. By the time they reached the foot of the stairs the storm was upon them and Kyle had to cover his ears to deaden the roar of the crowd gathered for the feast in a huge, cavernous hall.

Two long, trestle tables ran the length of the spacious hall, while a smaller, raised table stood at the back to form an elongated 'U'. Kyle saw King Bruide sitting in all his glory at the head of the high table, his gold crown glistening in the torch light, the voluminous sleeves of his fur-lined robe draped across the eating surface like a luxurious table cloth.

To the king's right were two empty seats. To his left sat the queen, short and dumpy, yet resplendent with jewels and looking just as radiant as her husband in a matching gown of the deepest purple silk. Her open, cheerful face was turned away from the king towards Jan and Megan, who looked very eye-catching in their cornflower blue gowns and neatly braided hair. While Jan charmed the queen with her childhood innocence, Megan listened with feigned interest to avoid having to converse with her portly neighbor on the left. She covered her left ear to drown out his raucous laughter, which rose above the endless din.

King Bruide was looking rather bored but suddenly came to life when he noticed Kyle and Lumpy, moving along the perimeter of the hall towards the high table. With one thunderous clap he silenced the crowd and, throughout the room, everyone seemed to hold their breath in anticipation until Kyle took his place beside the king and Lumpy occupied the seat next to him.

"Let the feast begin!"

Once again the king clapped his hands and the hall erupted.

To the din of conversation was added the clatter of dishes and the patter of bare feet as more than a dozen elves, displaying an uncanny resemblance to Ewewyrd, rushed into the hall bearing gleaming gold trays laden with steaming bowls. Close on their heals came a second wave of elves, appearing just as haggard as the first and visibly struggling with the oversized golden pitchers they had clenched in their small fists. As the elves scurried about distributing bowls and filling golden goblets,

Kyle couldn't help but notice the fear in their eyes. He saw the same worried look in Ewewyrd's eyes when first they met.

He was wondering what became of his friend when a pitcher appeared before his eyes. A bony arm shook under the strain of the heavy container and the grayish liquid threatened to spill onto the table long before it reached its intended target. To avoid a disaster, Kyle moved his goblet closer and braced the unsteady pitcher. When the goblet was brimming he turned his head to say "thank you" and couldn't believe his eyes.

"Ewewyrd?"

The servant gasped. Then she glanced around nervously to see if anyone had noticed. But with so many voices echoing off the hard stone walls it was virtually impossible for anyone other than Lumpy or King Bruide to have overheard. Luckily, the king had his face in a bowl and was making too much noise slurping the contents, while Lumpy was too busy stuffing his own mouth to even care about what was going on around him. The elf threw Kyle a warning glance before filling Lumpy's goblet and rushing away.

Kyle knew he made a mistake as soon as he opened his mouth. While the servant and the shepherd had many things in common, Ewewyrd's hardened face lacked many of the delicate features displayed by the serving girl's countenance. Not only that, the last time he saw Ewewyrd, the elf was nearly bald. This was hardly the case with the servant. Kyle wondered who the girl was and why she was so distraught by the mere mention of the shepherd's name. Perhaps they were brother and sister—or boyfriend and girlfriend. He cast aside these thoughts when a bowl was placed in front of him and he caught a whiff of the contents. Mushroom chowder. His empty stomach grumbled in protest.

Suddenly, a commotion at the far end of the hall helped him forget about the chowder; at least for the moment.

"You useless, good for nothing elf," snarled Loki. "Can't you do anything right?" He kicked at a trembling figure cowering at his feet.

The elf squealed even though Loki's foot only hit air.

A chorus of cheers encouraged Loki to try again, but before he had time to swing his foot the elf dove under the trestle table. The cheers turned to a chant. "Kill! Kill! Kill!" And on both sides bloodthirsty goblins kicked under and pounded on top of the table. Now and again a squeal emerged and seemed to excite the crowd further. Eventually the squeals ceased and the goblins quickly lost interest. Exhausted after their labors, they returned to their goblets and bowls, slurping and snorting like pigs at a trough.

Kyle noticed that Lumpy had drained his bowl and was looking around for more. So, while his friend's head was turned the other way, Kyle switched the bowls. He thought he had seen the last of the disgusting broth, but when King Bruide noticed the empty bowl in front of Kyle he snapped his fingers and, lo and behold, another piping hot bowl full to the brim appeared out of thin air. The empty bowl was whisked away just as cleverly.

Besides the mushroom chowder, which Kyle had to force down, the rest of the food was surprisingly delicious. Of the six courses that followed, the roast boar or 'razorback', as it was referred to by the goblins, was the most memorable, carted whole before the king and his guests. Its long, pointed tusks and jagged back armor were a testament to the boar's ferocious reputation. Kyle overheard the queen tell Jan that no less than the king himself had tracked down and killed the beast.

By the time the last platter had been removed and the acrobats tumbled into the hall, Kyle was ready to explode. And he hadn't even come close to cleaning every plate. That honor was reserved for the likes of Lumpy and King Bruide who, aside from spitting a few words in Kyle's direction, wolfed down everything put in front of them. At least Jan and Queen Windermere had more sense and consumed just enough to satisfy their hunger and not stuff themselves to the point of feeling sick. Megan ate sparingly, picking fussily at every dish, and gladly handing her leftovers to the gluttonous fellow on her left. It was much better to keep his mouth busy chewing on food than on her ear.

The acrobats amazed the crowd with their skill, strength and agility, making colossal pyramids out of their lithe bodies and leaping with lightning speed through golden rings of fire not much wider than the broadest shoulders. At one point they were moving so fast, tumbling and diving and leapfrogging over each other, that it was hard to follow all the action and any attempt to do so only made one dizzy. Then, as quickly as they appeared, they disappeared, to thunderous applause and cheers.

The acrobats were followed by jugglers, minstrels, a strongman and a magician, who mystified and enthralled the crowd with his tricks. Throughout much of his performance the room was so quiet you could have heard a pin drop. Only when the fellow had finished weaving his magic did the room explode. When he finally departed he left the crowd staring after him in awe—but only briefly. Soon, heads turned to neighbors and tongues started wagging as everyone who thought they knew the magician's secret was anxious to voice their opinion.

Satisfied that the feast and the entertainment that followed had been an overwhelming success the king turned to Kyle and said, "I know you are eager to leave but before you go it is only proper that we pay our respects to Odin."

Kyle didn't know who "Odin" was, but if the king wanted them to pay their respects, then who was he to argue; especially after showing them such a wonderful time. He only hoped it wouldn't take too long. As he thought about what he was going to say to his parents, the king raised his arms, silencing the crowd with an imperious clap of his hands.

At the first sign that the king was preparing to get up the gloomy attendant appeared out of nowhere to pull his chair away from the table. Automatically, everyone sitting at the lower tables stood as one and snapped to attention.

Upon stepping down from the high table the king offered his hand to the queen. She hesitated for a moment, then she hoisted her bulk out of the chair she seemed to be stuck in and accepted his assistance with a pleasant smile.

Hand in hand, the royal couple strolled through the crowd, nodding their heads from time to time and smiling half-heartedly at one and all as they guided their guests towards the main exit at the far end of the hall.

Along the way Kyle saw the elf, who had taken refuge under the trestle table, slinking towards the exit, as well. He observed her off and on through a forest of legs and followed her progress as she proceeded on a course parallel to the king and queen. Fearing that the king's party would arrive ahead of her and foil her escape, the elf sped up in a desperate attempt to reach the exit first. For a moment it looked as if the poor girl was going to get away unscathed, but she quickly lost the advantage when she got tangled up in her tattered gown and did a belly flop on the floor. Her startled cry did not go unnoticed.

The thing that stuck out in Kyle's mind as he quitted the hall was the roguish smile on one of the goblin faces. An agonizing squeal and roars of laughter followed the king and his party out into the corridor.

7
ODIN'S GIFT

As THE KING and queen led their guests along the marble foyer, they passed by the stairs leading down to the kitchen. From the clatter of dishes emanating from the narrow passage below Kyle knew that the elves were busy cleaning up after the feast. He felt the tightness in his stomach and was overcome by guilt. He had an urge to speak out against the unfairness he observed but feared his words might make life even more unbearable for the unfortunate elves. He kept his thoughts to himself, letting the patter of feet drown out the sounds of injustice.

The guards posted outside the great hall snapped to attention as the king's party strode past them. Whether it was out of fear or respect, Kyle had to admit that King Bruide had a firm grip on all his loyal subjects. Then he recalled the comment made by Rydd, about not giving a fig what the king likes or doesn't like, "It's Loki I aim to please." He pondered this in light of everything he had seen and heard and thought perhaps that not everyone was totally devoted to the king.

He began to wonder if Loki posed a threat to the king's authority but tossed the notion aside when he passed through a doorway at the opposite end of the foyer and was numbed by what he saw.

At first glance the entire room seemed to be aglow. Set ablaze by the flaming torches fastened to the walls. It took a moment to see beyond the illusion and realize that the room wasn't being consumed by flames but that it was loaded with gold. And the priceless works of art displayed on white marble pedestals or standing at random throughout the room were casting the fiery images; ornamental urns and vases, decorative goblets and plates, statues and figurines. More gold than Kyle could have ever imagined. He released the air he had been holding in behind an exclamation.

"Wow!"

Megan stepped past Kyle, cooing as she drifted over to the figure of a tearful unicorn bowing gracefully over a fallen warrior. While the warrior's body was marred by battle scars his face was a picture of serenity, for in his heart he believed in the unicorn's power to heal. Megan ran her fingers down the tear streaked face soaking up the lifelike droplets and symbolically transferring the gift of life from the unicorn to the warrior's battered, twisted body.

"Isn't it magnificent?" the king said, slipping away from the queen to stand alongside Megan. "The unicorn doesn't shed a tear for just anyone. Before receiving such an honor you must first earn a place in its heart. Only then will the unicorn grant you the gift of life."

The others had gathered around the statue as the king spoke.

Megan's lips quivered. "It's beautiful," she said in a quiet voice. "As soon as I stepped into the room I could feel myself being drawn towards it. I don't know why but…"

Her voice faltered as she felt her hand tingle; the same hand that had touched the statue. She rotated her wrist so the palm was facing upwards but, no matter how hard she gazed, she could not find anything that might have irritated the skin and caused such a sensation. Perplexed, she turned her hand over and over.

The king placed a reassuring hand on Megan's shoulder.

"You're not the first and you certainly won't be the last person to be overcome with emotion. The artist who molded and shaped the unicorn was a true master. He not only made the beast look real but he gave it life. Those tears are as real as you and I."

Megan re-examined the unicorn but saw nothing to suggest that it was anything more than a statue cast in gold.

"I'm not sure I understand," she said.

"Imagine a real unicorn. A living, breathing embodiment of the creature you see here. The unicorn's tears are flowing freely, bathing a mortally wounded warrior with the 'elixir of life'. Some of the teardrops are caught in a vessel. Now imagine the sculptor who created this masterpiece getting his hands on that vessel and mixing its contents with the gold that formed those tears. I'm not surprised you feel the way you do. Only, I would have expected the others to sense something, too. But then, perhaps not everyone has a heart as pure as yours."

The king raked Kyle, Lumpy and Jan with a critical eye.

Megan managed a nervous smile.

"I'm sure my friends feel the same way I do, but unlike me, they know how to keep their hands to themselves."

The king laughed heartily, his belly jiggling beneath the robe drawn tightly across his paunch.

"Well said! Let us move on before you paw everything in sight and some poor elf has to work through the night removing your greasy fingerprints."

At that, King Bruide steered around the statue and proceeded to walk towards a curtained opening at the far end of the room. While Kyle and Lumpy fell in step behind him, Queen Windermere attached herself to Jan, nattering away in her ear. Megan was still ensnared by the statue.

To say the queen was fond of Jan would be an understatement. Not only had she doted on the child during the feast, fussing over every little sneeze and making sure her goblet was always full and the plates that kept coming were hot and to her liking, but she kept eyeing her with affection. At the moment she was attempting to enlighten Jan, pointing out this and that and telling her the story behind some of the more striking exhibits as she led the younger girl on a circuitous route to the curtain.

Megan hurried to catch up with Jan and the queen once she managed to break the spell and drag herself away from the statue. She arrived just in time to hear Queen Windermere say, "Sometimes I think it's a curse but I don't know where we'd be without Draupner."

The look of incredulity in Jan's eyes made Megan wish she had arrived sooner. And, although she was hoping to hear more, the queen didn't say anything further about Draupner or a possible curse. In fact, the queen clammed up as soon as she noticed Megan was within earshot. Coincidence or not, Megan felt slighted and poked Jan in the ribs to get her attention after the queen followed the king and the boys through a gap between the curtain and the wall.

"What was that all about?" asked Megan.

"What was what all about?" said Jan bemused.

Jan had been listening so intently to the queen she had no idea that Megan had just joined them.

"That Draupner thing."

"Oh, that."

Jan was about to explain but before she could say another word the queen's stentorian voice ripped through the curtain.

"Are you coming, my dear?"

Whether Jan was coming or not, a stubby, ring-studded hand appeared out of nowhere and yanked her through the concealed gap in the wall. Frustrated, Megan stifled a groan and followed.

The room off the gallery was long and narrow with workbenches and storage shelves covering every available inch of space. Torches burned with such abundance that the chamber had a heavenly glow to it, but once again this was due to the preponderance of gold employed by the dwarfs, also known as dark elves, stationed at the workbenches.

Despite their aversion to light, the dwarves needed to see clearly to chisel and hammer the intricate details in their ornate works of art. From the tiniest trinket a child might enjoy to a massive breastplate fit for a king. They were richly rewarded for their efforts otherwise they would have never abided the light.

An unusually ugly dwarf, for all dwarfs were ugly, misshapen creatures, saw the king approaching and dropped what he was doing. Then he hobbled the width of the room and swung a breastplate embossed with the royal insignia off a shelf adjacent to the only exit. The king had to hold up abruptly or he would have slammed into the piece of armor.

"What does your Highness think of this?" said the dwarf.

His twisted smile revealed black stumps for teeth.

Unlike the goblins who revered the king or the elves who feared him, the dwarfs thought of themselves as equals, much to the king's dismay. Disguising his contempt behind a disarming smile King Bruide stepped back to make it seem like he wanted to take a closer look, although he really only wanted to distance himself from the dwarf's foul smelling breath.

"You've outdone yourself this time, Brokk. I'll have to find something special to please your palate when the entire suit is finished."

The dwarf licked his ulcerous lips.

"Just you make sure you do, your Highness. Just you make sure you do."

Returning the breastplate, Brokk turned his twisted body away from the king and hobbled back to his workbench.

None of the other dwarfs even bothered to look up. The only thing they cared about was their work and the tasty flesh that came their way whenever a job was completed.

The king clenched his fists and muttered under his breath.

"Pompous fool! I'd wrench his neck if I knew it would straighten him out."

Kyle observed Brokk bent over his work once again and noted that it would take a lot more than a simple flick of the wrist to get all the kinks out of the dwarf's gnarled, twisted back. He turned away quickly when the dwarf glanced over his shoulder and sneered at him.

The permanent scowl deepened as Brokk watched Kyle and the others exit.

Other than the dungeon, each of the rooms Kyle had been in throughout the palace were relatively comfortable, set at just the right temperature to counteract the dampness of the stone edifice. But as soon as he stepped inside the adjoining room he longed for the comfort of the cold, damp dungeon. There was only one other time he felt the way he did now and that was during the holidays when his parents persuaded him to try out the sauna in a hotel they were staying at. He remembered not being able to breathe then, and the feeling wasn't any different now as the fierce heat given off by a huge forge built into one of the walls threatened to suffocate him. To make matters worse, chemical odors of competing pungency mingled with the enduring smell of sweat.

A troll with a head, and no doubt a brain, much too small for its humungous, doughy body stood to one side of the forge chained to the wall. The shackles that bound both legs confined the sweaty, frothy beast to a corner of the room that allowed it to do little more than feed the forge from a stockpile of coal. Wrist fetters fastened to a short iron chain prevented the troll from swinging the coal shovel freely and pummeling the ill-tempered goblin standing just out of reach, teasing him with a whip.

The crack of the whip made everyone but the king jump.

"More fuel! More fuel!" the whip master hollered to be heard over the roar of the troll and the forge.

The troll kept grabbing at the air but it was just too slow and stupid too take hold of the whip. The goblin lashed out relentlessly until the beast picked up the shovel, dug into the coal pile and stoked the fire.

Nearby, a dwarf, drenched in sweat, was busy piling gold rings into an iron cauldron, hanging from a mobile winch that could be rolled in and out of the forge with relative ease. Each ring was about four inches in diameter, indistinguishable from the next and bearing a distinct resemblance to the rings embroidered on the king's robe. In addition to the mound at the dwarf's feet, more rings, thousands in fact, were heaped against the wall on the other side of the room. Numerous iron casts and metal worker's tools were scattered throughout, on the floor or atop work tables.

As if the room wasn't hot enough already, the extra coal managed to crank up the heat even more. It was just the right temperature for melting solid gold or anyone foolish enough to stand around watching. Kyle breathed a sigh of relief when the king made a beeline for an egress along the far wall.

On approaching the exit it was difficult to say who was making more noise. The tormented troll or the snoring guard slumped over a poleax in the next chamber. Puckering his brow in anger, the king snatched a mallet from a nearby table, swung his arm in a wide arc and clunked the guard over the head, all in one motion.

"Clank!"

The poleax shot out of the guard's hands and clattered to the floor.

"Hey! What's the big idea?" the guard said, tugging on the helmet that had slipped over his eyes then whirling around to challenge his attacker. "Your Highness!" he gasped.

His knees buckled almost as an afterthought to being whacked over the head.

"Perhaps you'd like to trade places with your friend in there," King Bruide said slowly, deliberately.

The guard's mouth opened and closed like a fish gasping for oxygen.

The king stood so close he could smell the man's fear. Snarling in his ear he said, "Pick up your weapon and don't let me see you or hear of you sleeping on duty again!"

"Yes your Highness. I mean no your Highness," the guard said, sounding like a blithering idiot.

"Now!"

The guard dropped to his knees and fumbled about nervously on the floor. Meanwhile, the king urged his guests forward by inviting them to join him before a colossal, white marble statue of Odin; the chief deity and god of wisdom, war and the dead in Norse mythology who sacrificed an eye for the privilege of drinking from Mimir, the fountain of wisdom.

"Gather around and don't be shy," the king said. "We're here to venerate Odin, not to cower in fear at his overwhelming magnificence."

The statue's magnificence was made richer by a dazzling gold throne.

Once they got over the initial shock Kyle and his companions spread out, arranging themselves around the king and queen much like they did during the feast. As Kyle and Lumpy moved into position they caught a glimpse of the only other object in the secluded room; a marble pedestal not unlike those in the gallery. They had to look twice to make sure what they saw on display on the pedestal was in fact there. Convinced that their eyes weren't deceiving them, they shrugged their shoulders and exchanged puzzled looks.

When everyone was standing in more or less a straight line the king bowed his head. He waited for the others to do likewise before extending his arms like a priest giving a sermon. Then he addressed the statue.

"Odin. King of the Aesir. Ruler of Asgard. God of wisdom and war. Cast your benevolent light upon our humble guests so that they may find their way home. And..."

The king paused briefly at the sound of a loud clank.

"...And grant them the benefit of your wisdom..." Two more clanks followed in rapid succession but this time the king hardly missed a beat. "...so that when they do return home and questions are asked, they have a clear understanding that ours is a secret world and must remain so forever in the eyes of man."

By the time King Bruide was through saying what he had to say there were eight distinct clanks in all.

If Lumpy hadn't witnessed it with his own eyes then he wouldn't have thought it possible. But from the second clank he paid less attention to what the king was saying and more attention to the gold ring on the pedestal. When he first set eyes on the ring he thought, "What is that thing doing there?" So did Kyle, perhaps, since the ring didn't look any different than the countless rings he saw scattered about in the other room. Well, now he knew. And he also had a better idea of where all those gold rings in the other room came from, and why there was no shortage of gold throughout the palace. What he didn't know was how. How a seemingly inanimate object could replicate itself, much like a strand of living DNA? He found himself asking the same question that was on Kyle's mind.

"How did it do that?"

The king raised his head. "Only the dark elves know the answer to that question. Draupner was their creation—their gift to Odin."

He broke ranks and moved towards the pedestal.

To get the queen's attention Jan tugged gently on her sleeve. "Our friend Ewewyrd is an elf."

The queen chortled. "He certainly is, my dear. But a lesser elf is hardly a dark elf." She regarded Jan's puzzled expression and patted her affectionately on the head. "Now, let's have no more talk of that meddlesome half breed."

The king was bending over one of the rings that had dropped from Draupner when the thought of Ewewyrd sent a sharp pain shooting down his spine. Grimacing and groaning, he snatched the ring with one hand and massaged his aching lower back with the other. His face was still twisted grimly when he stood to face everyone.

"That good for nothing elf doesn't even know Draupner exists," the king said angrily. "None of those worthless half breeds do. It belongs to us goblins."

Kyle's puzzled face was reflected in the ring the king was holding out in front of him.

"I don't understand. I thought you said the dark elves gave the ring to Odin? If that's true, then what is it doing here?"

"It was given as a gift to the goblin lord who fought alongside Odin during the mightiest battle of all time; Ragnarok—the day of doom. And every ninth night, as it has since the day Odin fell in battle, Draupner has rewarded the descendents of the goblins who perished by his side with eight gold rings, each as heavy and bright as the first. And now, just as you presented me with a gift, the gift of white light, I would like to offer this ring to you—as a memory of your visit. "

Stunned, Kyle reached out and took the gold ring; transfixed by its beauty, pleasantly surprised by its weight. Back home he would have had to exchange more than a hundred flashlights like the one he gave the king for this one ring. He gazed in awe at the generous gift, attempting to find the right words to say to express his gratitude. However, by the time he gathered his thoughts a commotion broke out in the other room and the king turned away suddenly and fled. It took him a moment to realize that he was standing alone. Everyone else, it seems, had rushed out after the king to see what all the fuss was about.

●   ●   ●   ●

By the time Kyle entered the room to join the others the coal dust and sparks were just beginning to settle, and any fight left in the troll, after obviously going berserk, went up the flue like smoke. Even so, the guard King Bruide had clobbered over the head a moment ago jabbed at the exhausted beast with his poleax to remind the troll that he was in charge now and no further disobedience would be tolerated.

Despite having ripped one of the leg restraints out of the wall the troll was happy to sit and rest among the hard lumps of coal and the pulverized remains the whip master. Kyle noticed the tip of the whip on the floor and followed a serpentine trail through the coal debris to a partially exposed hand. Much of the hand gripping the whip was buried under a ton or more of troll. The beast wasn't about to move from its perch even if the king offered to set it free.

Lumpy noticed the lifeless hand as well and edged forward to get a better look. Megan scrunched her face in disgust. Jan turned away, caught a glimpse of Kyle and screamed.

"There. There, child…Ah!" The queen paused, her eyes widening in sudden fear. She clutched her chest. "What have you done?" she demanded, staring at Kyle's marked right hand and pursing her lips in disapproval.

Kyle followed the queen's gaze and was horrified by what he saw. He dropped the ring, Draupner, as easily as he discarded King Bruide's generous gift.

Draupner hit the floor with a clank, bouncing once then rolling towards the jubilant troll. Before the ring rolled too far the king put out a foot to stop it. Then he leaned over and scooped it up. The look he gave Kyle was more oppressive than the heat.

8
DRAUPNER'S CURSE

"GUARDS!"

The king's booming voice rang out beyond the walls of the forge.

Kyle made a desperate attempt to wipe his hand clean of the crime but the sinister black mark on his fingers and thumb would not go away no matter how hard he rubbed. Neither would the black band on Draupner that marked the spot befouled by his unworthy hands. Despite the suffocating heat he found himself shivering behind the king's icy glare.

The sound of voices and heavy feet drew the attention away from Kyle; at least for the moment. However, any relief he may have felt was short-lived when Loki came charging into the room like a bull let loose in an arena. Not far behind him were Rydd and the two guards posted outside the great hall.

Loki gazed wide-eyed at Kyle's blemished right hand.

"I knew you were up to no good," he said, throwing Kyle at look of contempt.

Kyle tried to speak but his breath caught in his throat. The fact that his guilt was as plain as the nose on his face made it impossible to deny any wrongdoing.

"Take them to the dungeon," the king roared.

Loki bared his pointed teeth.

"With pleasure your Highness."

He lunged forward, gripping Kyle by the shoulder and fixing him with a vice-like grip. Then he reached across and seized Jan roughly by the scruff of the neck.

Startled, Jan shrieked.

"Unhand that child, now!" the queen screeched, tugging on Loki's arm.

Loki refused to let go, regarding the queen coolly and turning to the king for support.

"Your Highness?"

The king's mouth was set in a ferocious scowl.

"You heard me," he said. "Take them away! All of them."

The queen could see by the look in his eye that the king was seething with rage and any attempt to undermine his authority might prove disastrous for Jan and the others. She decided to let him have his way, but not before raising her eyes reprovingly at Loki and issuing a stern warning.

"Harm just one hair on that dear child's head and you will find yourself answering to me."

Loki knew better than to take the queen's warning lightly. Hiding behind an insincere smile he said, "I wouldn't dream of it my Lady."

As Loki turned away Jan saw the smile turn into a dark scowl.

Shooting Jan a warning glance, Loki pushed her and Kyle towards Megan and Lumpy. Then, Rydd and the two guards, along with Loki, surrounded the foursome and marched them out of the room.

●　　　●　　　●　　　●

Darkness reigned in the chilly damp cell, broken only by a sliver of light peeking through a gap between the door and the hard stone floor. The candle they were left with had burned out long ago, leaving them freezing and shivering in the dark. While Megan and Jan had huddled together on the spider infested floor and fallen asleep quickly, Kyle was too distraught to even consider taking a nap. Not only was he worried about the fate of each and every one of them but he had nagging concerns over his own well-being. The last time he looked the mark on his fingers and thumb had spread like cancer. And he was beginning to feel strange, slightly queasy, albeit not quite as nauseous as Lumpy who was about to discover that too much of anything, even good food, is not such a good thing.

An anguished moan, followed by the sound of retching, signaled the beginning of the great purge. Before he was through spilling his guts Lumpy went on to hurl three more times, leaving him worn out and exhausted. He collapsed in a heap, clutching his aching stomach and vowing to never overindulge again.

The smell of vomit permeated the cell, making Kyle gag and giving the spiders close to Lumpy and the mess he had just made a reason to head for the exit. Big and small, fat and spindly, the exodus was on. Kyle had his sights set on one particularly large specimen that was having no luck at all. Time and time again the arachnid managed to squeeze its plump, oversized body through the gap under the door, only to vanish briefly then reappear rather agitated. The last time through the spider didn't come back so Kyle was sure that it finally made good its escape. Then a shadow appeared in the gap and a loud pop on the other side of the door revealed the spider's fate.

Megan and Jan were startled awake by the sound of the bolt sliding back and the door creaking open. They turned up their noses in disgust as an acrid odor assaulted their delicate senses.

A boot appeared in the opening and the edge of the door was used to scrape the spider guts off the bottom of it. Kyle recognized the boot and shuddered.

"Alright, you worthless pile of sheep's dung," said Loki, barging into the cell and kicking at Kyle, "on your feet!"

He raised his foot as if to strike Jan, too, but one glimpse of her sweaty, feverish face set off warning bells. Recalling the queen's threat, he lowered his foot and barked, "Come on! We haven't got all day. The king wants to have a word with you four."

Loki turned abruptly to avoid Jan's pathetic gaze and stomped out of the cell, but not before putting the boots to Lumpy.

His departure was followed by a chorus of moans and groans.

•   •   •   •

Kyle stood before the king like a condemned man waiting to be sentenced; shoulders stooped, head hung in shame, forlorn expression on his face. To betray the king's trust was one thing. But to betray his friends for the sake of worldly wealth was another. The feeling of guilt weighing him down was almost too much bear. His knees buckled under the strain.

Loki cracked Kyle in the back with the hilt of his sword.

"Stand up straight when you're in the presence of the king!"

Kyle snapped to attention but lowered his head quickly when he found himself facing the king's stony glower. The angry frown seemed to be a permanent feature, unaltered since Loki and his two cronies, Rydd and Jorge, ushered Kyle and his companions into the great hall a few minutes earlier. Out of the corner of his eye he saw Ewewyrd, pale and silent, his eyes cast down.

With so much on his mind Kyle had completely forgotten Ewewyrd existed, so it came as somewhat of a surprise to see the elf standing alone, like some forsaken urchin, when they entered the great hall. Even more shocking were the bumps and bruises and patches of dried up blood on the elf's body and thread-bare clothes. Kyle thought that Jan looked rather ghastly until he caught a glimpse of Ewewyrd.

The uneasy quiet was shattered by the sound of a disturbance just beyond the open doors. Through all the shouting and scuffling of feet Brokk's haughty voice resonated loud and clear.

"If the king has something important to say let him come to me. I don't know why I—"

The shock of being catapulted backwards into the hall caught the pugnacious dwarf off guard. However, before he could resume protesting, the two guards who had taken him from his work, against his will, slammed the doors unceremoniously in his face. Not that it really mattered. He promptly rounded and focused his ire on the king himself.

"I demand to know what this is all about."

Seething with rage, Loki unsheathed his sword and pointed it menacingly at the insolent dwarf.

"Hold your tongue!"

Brokk jabbed his fists on his hips and jutted his jaw, daring Loki to strike him.

"Hold your own tongue, you slobbering buffoon."

"Silence!" the king shouted.

King Bruide's face suffused with color as he leaned forward and gripped the arms of the glistening throne. The blazing torch on the wall behind him illuminated him with an eerie glow. Pointing a stubby finger at Loki he said, "You! Put away that sword before you poke out someone's eye. And you, master smith, I'd advise you to keep a tight rein on that tongue of yours. Someday you're bound to slip on it and never get back up."

Loki grudgingly re-sheathed the sword. Meanwhile, Brokk's tense face seemed to relax as he chewed on the king's sage advice and the even dire hidden message.

The king flashed the ghost of a smile as he leaned back in his chair.

"Good!"

He wiggled his rump in an effort to make himself more comfortable. "Now, master smith, I apologize for taking you from your work but this is a matter of the utmost urgency that demands your immediate attention."

Brokk's jaw dropped. "But I—"

The king waved a placating hand.

"I know you are busy, working on my suit of armor no doubt, but let me continue. The sooner you hear what I have to say, the sooner you can leave."

The dwarf could tell from the determination in the king's voice that he wasn't going anywhere until he did indeed listen. Resigned to the fact, he bobbed his head and shut his mouth, hiding the black stumps that passed for teeth and making it easier for the king to endure his repellent, insolent mug.

With Brokk pacified, the king was ready to proceed. He snapped his fingers, reaching out to receive a ragged, sackcloth bag from the mournful attendant who was always by his side. Eying the crude bag, the contents of which left an unmistakable imprint in the palm of his hand, he was flooded with emotion as the severity of the sentence he was about to hand down weighed heavily on his royal conscience. A shadow of doubt seemed to pass over him like a wave. Then he gazed at Kyle's hand and he saw the black cancer growing, spreading before his very eyes, and he knew he was making the right decision.

He held up the bag for all to see.

"I hold in my hand a symbol of greed. Of dishonesty! Betrayal! Contempt for the law! All these things I see mirrored before me. And for what? A few ounces of gold?"

Appalled at the thought, he tossed the bag.

The bag flipped in the air and Draupner spilled out, clanking distinctly in the soundless room as it hit the carpeted floor before the empty sack. The ring wobbled across the carpet, coming to rest at Kyle's feet.

Kyle's eyes expanded in horror when he realized how much the black band had grown, doubling in size since he last saw the ring.

"Get used to it," said the king. "It'll only get uglier now that you have unleashed the curse."

"Curse!" exclaimed Megan.

"But of course," the king said dryly. "Draupner was a gift to the gods and from the gods. You don't honestly believe the dark elves would create such a treasure without providing some sort of protection to keep it from the likes of you." His calm voice dripped contempt. "Only Odin or the chosen one is allowed to touch the ring. And as a descendant of the goblin lord who fought alongside Odin, that privilege belongs to me. Anyone other than I who touches the ring, for whatever purpose, releases the curse at their own peril. As you can see, it's not a pretty sight."

Lumpy had been listening intently and was puzzled by what he had heard.

"But surely there's something you can do?"

The king shook his head.

"Regrettably, there is nothing I can do to save the ring or your friend. The putrefaction you see will continue for nine days until the disease spreads throughout and destroys them both. Only by seeking out and finding the descendants of Sindri and Brokk the Elder, the dark elves who created Draupner, can the ring be made pure again and the curse lifted. The candle has started burning and only you four can stop it from going out forever."

Jan uttered a pained moan and fainted.

Kyle wanted to rush to her side but Loki barred the way, rapping him hard with the blade of his sword. But that didn't stop the figure standing in the shadows and listening with interest from barging through a side entrance and scooping up the unconscious child.

The queen's voice quivered with rage as she whirled around to face the king.

"Do what you must but leave this child out of it. She's under my protection now."

She stomped away and nobody dared to stop her.

While Loki may have viewed Jan's sudden departure as somewhat of a disappointment, the king saw it differently. He had already discussed his decision at length with the queen and he was expecting her to intervene at some point in the proceedings to argue the girl's case further. Jan's collapse couldn't have come at a better time. Not only had he avoided a potentially embarrassing situation, one that would have surely undermined his authority, but he actually felt good about the outcome. He was thinking about how happy the child had made his queen when he noticed Ewewyrd standing off to the side. He was suddenly struck by an idea; one that would rid him of the bothersome elf once and for all.

The king pointed at Ewewyrd.

"I should have dealt with you more severely in the past, but you're the best darn shepherd I've got. No one else seems to have any success lambing and, since the dark elves are partial to lamb—" He paused to glance at Brokk. The dwarf ran his tongue along his upper lip as if the taste of lamb was on it. "—I've had to overlook your constant indiscretions."

Without warning the king raised his voice, making Ewewyrd jump. "But I'm not about to this time, elf. By meddling, you are just as responsible for what has happened as those two." He flicked his wrist at Megan and Lumpy. "So, to ensure you are sufficiently punished, I'm going to order you to accompany them."

Ewewyrd let out a piteous cry, made all the more pathetic by the distraught look in his blood-shot eyes. His knobby knees clacked together as his entire body began to quiver and shake uncontrollably.

King Bruide turned up his nose in disgust.

"Get him out of my sight before I change my mind and have him executed on the spot. And take them with you! I don't want to see their wretched faces again until Draupner has been restored to its former glory."

Loki clicked his heels together smartly.

"Yes your Highness."

He drew his sword, paddling Ewewyrd's backside and making the elf squeal. Then he waved the blade around to round up the rest of the condemned and hasten their departure from the great hall.

Brokk watched in stunned silence as they exited.

The king noticed a change in the habitually cantankerous dwarf and couldn't help but be amused. The legend of the curse was nothing new to Brokk, especially since he came from the same stock that created the ring, but to hear that it had been unleashed must have come as a shock.

"Now that you've heard what I have to say tell me truthfully, what chance, if any, do they have to succeed?"

Brokk scrunched up his ugly face.

"The dangers are many and varied, especially for ones so young and inexperienced. Even if they knew where they were going..."

"Ah! But that's where you can help. I want you to draw a map to show them the surest and safest route."

The dwarf searched his memory.

"I'll do my best but it's been many years since I made the journey. Darkalfheim is but a distant memory."

The king sensed a hint of sorrow in the dwarf's voice.

"Do you ever regret leaving its dark caverns and coming here to work for me?"

"I regret trading darkness for light and losing sight of ancient wisdom passed on by word of mouth since time immemorial. Other than that, there is always plenty to do in Midgard and no lack of fresh flesh after a hard days work."

"Eating seems to be an obsession with you. Why is that?"

"If there's one thing I'll never forget it's the pain of rising each morning knowing that my stomach would be as empty at the end of the day as it was when I first got out of bed."

The king nodded his head.

"I see. Well, if it is fresh flesh you want then it is fresh flesh you shall have—as soon as you deliver the map."

Brokk licked his lips expectantly.

"It'll be in your hands shortly. Not that it will make much difference. I fear they are doomed with or without it."

9

THE BLACK FOREST

WITHIN A MATTER of hours Kyle saw his fortune change twice. Unfortunately, the last time it changed was for the worse and there was nothing in the foreseeable future to suggest his luck would turn around once again. And just in case he was thinking otherwise, a not so gentle tug on the rope wrapped securely around his neck served as a reminder.

As soon as the condemned had been led out of the great hall, Loki made sure that Megan and Lumpy changed back into their damp clothes. Kyle, on the other hand, had to throw a dark, hooded cloak, much like a monk's habit, on over his wet pants and shirt to conceal the effects of the curse, which had spread to his other hand. All four, Ewewyrd included, were then strung together at the neck and paraded through the streets of Midgard like felons on the way to the gallows, in tow behind Loki on horseback.

Kyle wanted to slip a finger between the rope and his throat to prevent it from choking him but he was afraid someone might see his blackened hands. Or even worse, catch a glimpse of Draupner, fastened to a heavy metal chain and looped around his neck. Instead, he kept his hands buried deep inside the folds of the long, flowing sleeves and suffered like the others.

There was a sense of relief for Kyle and his companions when they approached the outer wall and the massive gates creaked open. The cacophony that filled the air came to a sudden halt, and the angry mob that had accompanied them most of the way dispersed without incident, leaving Loki, alone, to lead the condemned down the gentle slope to the stone bridge below.

"That's far enough," growled Loki, pulling on the reins and stopping the horse just short of the bridge.

He unwound the rope wrapped around the saddle and tossed the free end on the ground at Kyle's feet.

"I hope you choke yourself," he said mockingly.

Kyle gazed vacantly at the rope.

Loki treated Kyle to an unpleasant sneer. Then he spun the horse round and began to leave. But there was something he must have forgotten to do because he paused long enough to reach inside his doublet and produce a folded scrap of parchment.

"You might want to take a look at this," he said, his face widening in a vicious grin. "Not that it will do you any good. Not where you're going."

He tossed the parchment at Kyle.

The valley echoed with Loki's laughter as Kyle bent down to retrieve the parchment. Upon unfolding it, he was surprised to see it was a map.

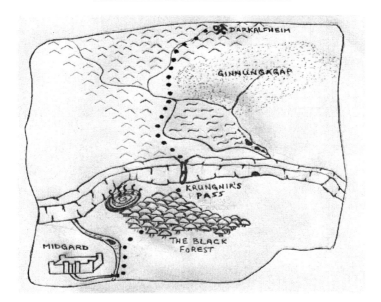

Lumpy rested a hand on Kyle's shoulder and peered at the crude map.

"Well, at least now we know where we're going."

Kyle gagged as an unsavory blend of body odor and vomit assaulted his nose. To distance himself from Lumpy's foul smelling T-shirt and the clots of barf still clinging to his hair, Kyle drifted towards Ewewyrd. He held out the map so that the elf could make out the details.

"What do make of this?" said Kyle.

The elf's pupils dilated as he followed the dotted line from the spot on the river where they were presently standing to a cluster of mushroom shapes identified as the 'Black Forest'. By the time his eyes came to the area marked 'Krungnir's Pass' he was trembling and blubbering like an idiot. Beads of sweat sprung to life, rolling down his balding head and trickling across deep furrows on his forehead and his haggard face.

Megan threw up her arms in despair.

"Good grief! If that's what looking at a harmless map can do, I'd hate to see what happens when he really gets scared."

Kyle put a comforting hand on Ewewyrd's shoulder.

"I know you're not looking forward to this. None of us are. But we need you to be strong. That's the only way we're going to make it. Isn't that right, Megan?" He frowned critically at her.

Contrite, Megan nodded in agreement.

It's never easy for a certified coward to put on a brave face but somehow Ewewyrd managed to pull himself together and take another look at the map. Taking a deep breath he said, "Do you want me to tell you what I know for certain or what I believe to be true? It won't take long either way."

"Why don't you start with what you know for certain," said Kyle encouragingly.

"If we leave now we should be able to reach the forest by nightfall."

"Nightfall!" exclaimed Lumpy. "How the heck can you possibly tell when it's nighttime around here?"

He gazed skyward, rubbing his chin thoughtfully.

Ewewyrd eyed Lumpy strangely. "It gets dark."

It was such a simple response yet it left Lumpy even more perplexed. For the first time he observed his surroundings with an open mind, but the orange glow that permeated the air didn't seem to originate from anywhere in particular, so it was impossible to imagine how such a phenomenon might occur in the absence of a sun or some other celestial body that rose and fell with the passing of each day. Not wanting to waste any more time mulling over it he said, "Of course. Why didn't I think of that?" There was a hint of sarcasm in his voice.

Kyle regarded Lumpy severely before questioning Ewewyrd further.

"What else can you tell us, Ewewyrd?"

The elf shrugged his scrawny shoulders. "Nothing—I've only been out of the valley once and that was when one of the lambs wandered into the forest and got lost."

A dark shadow seemed to pass over him and he suddenly became quiet.

Eager to hear more Kyle said, "Did you find it?"

Ewewyrd's lips quivered and his voice trembled when he spoke. "Oh, I found it alright—what was left of it, at least. After that I didn't go near the forest again."

"That's horrible," gasped Megan.

"It was terrible," said Ewewyrd shivering. "So now that you know how dangerous the forest can be you'll believe me when I say—" He paused as a rickety old cart rumbled across the bridge towards the gates, leaving a cloud of coal dust in its wake. Once the coal dust had settled and everyone had stopped coughing he continued. "—if we put so much as one foot in that forest, it will be the last thing we do. The same thing will happen to us that happened to that poor lamb."

Megan shuddered at the thought.

Lumpy's mocking snort was drowned out by the creaking gates as they closed behind the cart.

"Do you actually believe all this nonsense? Can't you see he's only trying to scare us? Although why he'd want to do that is beyond me." He eyed Ewewyrd suspiciously.

"It's true!" said Ewewyrd. "And if you have any sense you'll take my advice and go around the forest, like this." He outlined the way with his finger, skirting the woods but taking the longer of two possible routes. "It's the only way to go with the lava pits blocking the way here." He drew an imaginary circle around the oval-shaped blob to the left of the forest.

Lumpy gave a short bark of laughter.

"And while we're at it why don't we take in some of the sights. We're not in a hurry. Are we Kyle?"

"Lumpy has a point," said Kyle. "We haven't got time to go that way even if we wanted to."

"But we can make time," pleaded Ewewyrd.

Kyle shook his head.

"Not enough. You just said that we'd be lucky to reach the forest before it gets dark. Assuming we get through the forest tomorrow, that would bring us to the pass the following evening." He paused to study the map. "The route you outlined is three times further. We can't afford to waste that much time."

Lumpy slung a beefy arm over Kyle's shoulders and steered him towards the bridge.

"And we'll have even less time to waste if we don't stop talking and put our butts in gear."

As Lumpy guided Kyle across the bridge, Megan and Ewewyrd fell in step behind them.

•   •   •   •

They followed the river downstream for nearly two hours, keeping up the brusque pace established by Lumpy from the onset. Other than a few sheep, that must have wandered off and got lost, they came across nothing of interest until they reached the sharp bend indicated on the map. It was at this point that the river broadened to accommodate a small island. Standing on the island was a haphazard collection of shabby stone, daubed with mud, huts. Although there was no one to be seen, smoke and cooking odors drifted out of the open roofs to reveal where everyone was hiding. A distraught ewe bleated at them through a sizeable gap in a makeshift wooden fence.

"I wouldn't doubt it if that's one of mine," said Ewewyrd sadly. "They always seem to go missing near here."

He dipped his hands in the river and scooped out a handful of water, slurping it down and smacking his lips.

Assured that the water was drinkable, Megan crouched down and cupped her hands, running them through the gurgling river and raising them overflowing to her mouth. As soon as the cool liquid touched her lips she spat it out.

"How can you drink that?" she said, pulling a face. "It tastes disgusting."

Simultaneously, Kyle and Lumpy sampled the river. No sooner had the water touched their lips than they spewed it out, as well.

Ewewyrd downed another mouthful of the brackish water before offering them this sage advice.

"It may not taste very good but you'll be glad you made the sacrifice when you don't see another drop of the stuff for days."

An image of the map appeared in Kyle's head.

"Ewewyrd's right. This may be the last water we see for quite some time."

"How long?" said Megan with a sigh.

"Two—maybe three days," said Kyle uncertainly. He really had no idea how long it would take but he didn't want Megan to know. "Assuming the map is drawn to scale it should take us that long to reach the sea beyond that pass."

"In that case," said Lumpy, "I'm going to take as much water with me as I can."

He leapt in the river, disappearing in a huge plume of water that rained down on Kyle and Ewewyrd.

Megan burst out laughing.

When Lumpy resurfaced he saw Megan enjoying the moment and a mischievous grin broke through the shower of water he appeared through. Kicking at the water and paddling towards shore, he stood where the river was waste deep and splattered her until she was just as wet as Kyle and Ewewyrd.

Now that they were soaked, Kyle and Megan jumped in the river too and for the next few minutes Ewewyrd leaned back on the spongy ground and watched them splash about as if they didn't have a care in the world. When they were finally done playing, all three of them had managed to swallow enough of the salty water to get them through the rest of the day.

With their spirits lifted, they proceeded towards the Black Forest, looming dark and forbidding in the distance.

•   •   •   •

By the time they reached the forest the orange tinted sky had somehow lost its luster, reducing everything around them to shadows. Luckily there was just enough light for them to see each other, and the outline of a trail cut deep into the dense underbrush and the compact, mushroom-shaped trees towering above them. The twisted, disfigured limbs of the bushes that sprang up along the trail shuddered in response to a sudden gust of wind. The air that arrived with it was cool and smelled musty.

Kyle and Megan shivered as the icy breeze passed through their damp clothes and chilled them to the bone. Ewewyrd trembled and his knees knocked out of fear. Lumpy was too thick skinned to feel either the cold or fear.

"Do you feel that breeze?" said Lumpy, inhaling deeply, pleasurably. "I'll bet you anything it's coming from that huge body of water on the other side of the pass. All we have to do is stay on this trail and we'll be there before you know it."

"You make it sound so easy," said Megan. "Somehow I don't think we will be that lucky."

"That's what I like about you, Megan," said Lumpy. "You're always so optimistic."

"I can't help thinking about that poor lamb."

Lumpy's stomach growled, making Ewewyrd jump.

"Would you rather we stay here and slowly die of hunger?" he said. "I, for one, prefer a quick death to a slow and painful one."

"I'd rather not have the choice," said Kyle irritably. His right hand was itching something fierce but he resisted the urge to scratch it. "But since I do, is it asking too much to keep your mouth shut—unless, of course, you plan on announcing our arrival to all the creatures living in the forest."

His soggy sneakers squeaked as he turned away from the others and plodded into a maze of darkness.

Megan ran after Kyle. But not before elbowing Lumpy in the stomach and calling him an oaf. Lumpy released a belly full of air that seemed to catch hold of Ewewyrd and propel him forward into the dreaded forest.

They walked in silence, their eyes to the ground, their ears straining for the faintest sound. Shortly after entering, they reached a fork in the path and, without hesitation, Kyle headed right. The others followed blindly.

Before long, the forest began to close in on them and they had to duck under and side-step the overhanging branches and shrubs that tried to reclaim the land. To avoid poking out an eye they trod carefully, proceeding much slower than they would have preferred; but even that didn't stop them from being stung by the occasional prickly vine, hanging down like a ghostly tendril and nearly invisible in the waning light.

Megan could swear she heard voices so she kept glancing around, and while she never saw anything definite, she had the terrible feeling they were being watched. At one point she looked up suddenly and saw a branch move. She was about to make her suspicions known to the others when Kyle halted without warning at the edge of a clearing and she ploughed into him.

The collision left her breathless and speechless—but only for a moment. "Did you see that?" she whispered, her startled gaze fixed to the quivering bush on the far side of the clearing.

Kyle saw the bush flutter too. He held a finger to his lips to shush Megan. Then, he muttered something in Lumpy's ear and the two of them began to circle the clearing from opposite directions.

As they approached the bush a twig snapped, loud and clear in the stillness of the night. They stood motionless, holding their breath and watching the bush for any sign of movement. When nothing happened they continued, treading lightly, careful not make a sound. They edged closer, preparing to launch an assault when a bloodcurdling scream cut through the darkness like a knife.

"Freyja!" exclaimed Ewewyrd.

Without hesitation, the elf spun round and fled back down the trail.

Kyle and Lumpy held up for a second, giving their prey just enough time to make good its escape. Holding nothing but broken branches and air between them, they turned their attention to the frantic cries of a female in distress.

"Help me, Ewewyrd! Help..."

A shrill screech and silence followed the plea for help.

"I'm coming, Freyja," shouted Ewewyrd, his voice uncommonly fearless.

Kyle, Lumpy and Megan heard Ewewyrd crashing through the undergrowth, so they had no problem tracking him down. When they finally caught up with him, just beyond the point where the path forked to the left, he was lying on his stomach with his arms outstretched and his hands clasped around a bony arm almost entirely submerged in mud. Despite all the grunting and groaning, he was making no progress. In fact, the limb sank deeper and deeper as the weight at the other end pulled him towards the mire.

Lumpy rushed over to assist Ewewyrd, pinning his legs to the ground to prevent him from sliding any further. Meanwhile, Kyle dove and grabbed the limb just as it slipped out of the elf's hand. Ewewyrd watched in horror as Kyle reached in and plucked a limp body out of the suffocating, sucking mud.

Megan's hands flew to her mouth and her eyes became round with alarm. "Is she dead?" She noted the similarity between the rags Ewewyrd was wearing and the victim's tattered, muddy dress.

Kyle's solemn expression seemed to say, "Yes".

Ewewyrd rose to his knees and crawled over to the mud-caked body. As the tears began to flow, he reached down and picked up a lock of brown hair, stroking it with his thumb, rubbing it against his wet cheek. Then he allowed the lock to slip away before pressing his hands against his downcast face and letting out a piteous wail.

"What have I done?".

Tears welled up in Megan's eyes as she was overcome by grief. Sharing the elf's sorrow, she dropped to her knees and placed a soothing arm around his hunched shoulders, caressing him gently. Kyle tried to hold back the tears but he fought a losing battle. Only Lumpy's eyes remained unclouded long enough to see a pair of bulging eyeballs poke big, round holes in the mud.

The mud crumbled away as a broad smile carved a deep rift in the facial mask. "You saved me," the elf maiden said, gazing adoringly at Ewewyrd.

When he heard her sweet voice, Ewewyrd's head shot up and his face broke into a beam of pleasure. Then, he recalled how he had actually failed. He hung his head in shame, fidgeting nervously in the silence that followed.

Kyle didn't want to disillusion the girl so he put on an ingenuous face and lied through his teeth.

"You should have seen him tear through the forest when he heard you cry out. Why, he got here so fast, by the time we arrived, there was nothing for us to do but watch in awe as he grabbed hold of your arm just as you were going to slip away forever and pulled you out of the mud."

There was a shadow of doubt on the maiden's face so Megan decided to stretch the truth even further.

"I never saw anything so amazing in all my life. Who would have thought such a puny little person—elf—could be so strong."

"Not me. That's for sure," jeered Lumpy.

Choosing to ignore Lumpy's snort of derision, Freyja sat upright unexpectedly, swung her muddy arms around Ewewyrd's neck and planted a soggy kiss on his lips.

"Yuck!"

Lumpy turned away, making a disgusting face.

Ewewyrd thought his neck was going to snap and was actually relieved when Freyja finally released her grip. He fell backwards in a swoon, with splotches of mud clinging to his face and ears.

Kyle observed the face behind the mud and thought there was something about it that looked familiar.

"Haven't I seen you before," he asked.

The elf maiden smiled, recalling the kindness he had shown her the last time they met.

"I was the one who filled your goblet," she said with a snicker. "The one you mistakenly thought was Ewewyrd."

Kyle snapped his fingers. "That's right. You almost poured the contents of the pitcher onto the table instead of into my glass."

She bowed her head. "I never did get to thank you," she said ashamedly.

"It wasn't necessary. That pitcher was way too heavy and awkward for your—" He stared at her scrawny arms.

"Bony arms," she offered. She extended one of the limbs and introduced herself. "My name is Freyja. And you must be Kyle." Suddenly, a grave expression clouded her bright face. "I heard what happened to you. All of you—" She glanced at everyone in turn. "—and I wanted to help."

"But how did you escape?" wondered Megan. "I would have thought it was impossible with all those creepy goblins walking about everywhere."

Freyja waggled a mud-spattered sheepskin pouch. It was fastened to a length of rope that was wrapped around her slender waist. "I used Ewewyrd's magical fairy dust."

She gazed at Ewewyrd, lighting up the dark forest with another one of her award winning smiles.

"Do you have any left?" asked Ewewyrd.

She shook the pouch and it rustled lightly.

"Good," Ewewyrd said, uttering a sigh of relief. "I'm sure we're going to eventually need it."

Lumpy regarded Freyja more closely, trying to see through all the mud caked on her body.

"You didn't by any chance bring anything else with you? Like food, perhaps."

"As a matter of fact I did."

She saw Lumpy's eyes widen expectantly and she suddenly felt bad. "Unfortunately, the bag it was in must have fallen in the bog. I don't see it around here anywhere."

Disappointed, Lumpy scanned the surface of the quagmire. He didn't see what he was looking for but what he did see chilled him to the bone. "Ah…!" He gazed across the muddy expanse with eyes dilated in fear.

"It's not the end of the world," said Megan. "I'm sure we will find something else to eee..." She uttered a scream that would have done a banshee proud.

The razorback posted on the other side of the quagmire raised its formidable tusks in the air and screeched to wake the dead. Frustrated by the impassable sea of mud, it paced back and forth, snorting and pawing at the ground.

Kyle sprung to his feet.

"We better get out of here before that thing realizes it's a lot easier to go around than through the bog."

No sooner had the words left his mouth than the beast vented its anger on the bushes penning it in. The sound of snapping branches split the air.

The idea of an encounter with the fearsome beast was enough to spur Megan into action, and even her trembling legs couldn't stop her from dashing away as fast as humanly possible. She took to her heels, tearing blindly past the trees and shrubs that lined the path. In her haste, she unwittingly covered their previous tracks, winding up at the clearing.

As she came upon open ground she stopped to catch her breath and look around for a safe haven. Stale, hot breath gusted on to the back of her neck and she knew Lumpy was right behind her. She could hear the others crashing through the forest not far away, as well as the roars and grunts of the razorback. It must have broken through the underbrush and stumbled onto the path.

"Keep moving," shouted Kyle from the back of the pack. "It's right behind me."

Megan could feel the weight of the others pressing against her, urging her forward, but there was nowhere to run and nowhere to hide once she led them into the clearing. They would be easy targets for the razorback's stabbing, ripping tusks. She was close to tears when muffled voices and movement in the overhanging branches attracted her attention. All of a sudden, several knotted vines fell from the trees and dangled in midair only a hop and a skip away. Without further delay, she ran into the clearing, snatched the first vine she came to and clambered to safety.

Lumpy saw what Megan was up to when he burst onto the scene but the first vine he tugged on broke in his hands with a twang. As he fell heavily, Ewewyrd and Freyja vaulted over his prostrate body and scaled a pair of vines before he had even budged. By the time he got back on his feet, Kyle rushed into the clearing with the snorting razorback close on his heels.

The razorback lowered its head and charged, but Kyle managed to grab a vine and swing out of the way just before being skewered. As he started to climb, the enraged beast slashed at the swinging vine with its tusks. It was so busy taking its frustration out on the vine that it failed to notice Lumpy, standing only a few feet away. By the time the beast saw him it was too late. It snorted in disgust. Then it flopped on the ground and watched Lumpy struggle up one of the crude ropes hoping, perhaps, that the thin vine would snap and deliver a hearty meal.

●   ●   ●   ●

The queen sat on the edge of a bed piled high with blankets and dabbed at Jan's sweaty face with a cold, damp cloth. Despite the fever gripping her body, Jan shivered in her sleep, prompting the queen to drop the cloth in a washbasin and to pull the blankets further up under her chin, until all that showed was her pallid face. The whiteness of her skin contrasted sharply with the red, blue and green of the queen's bejeweled hands, and its waxy sheen made her face look more like a death mask than the real thing.

A candle on a table next to the bed sputtered as the flame danced over a puddle of wax. The queen lit another candle before it fizzled and died, praying that not too much more wax would have to melt before the fever finally broke.

●   ●   ●   ●

Branches slashed at Kyle's face and arms as he scrambled up the vine, desperate to put as much distance as possible between himself and the fearsome creature below. He tried not to think of the pain each time he grasped the makeshift rope because it was nothing when compared to the hurt he had to carry around inside. Through a tangle of branches he saw the limb securing the vine and hastened to reach it before his hands became much rawer. Reaching up, he clutched the branch and managed to pull himself to safety.

Winded, he clung to the branch, his face pressed against the rough bark. Through his own pounding heart he heard Lumpy struggling below and was about to offer some words of encouragement when something touched his shoulder. He started in surprise.

A hairy arm shot out and grasped the cloak, stopping him from falling.

"No need be scared," came a squeaky voice. "Saffron be friend. Save you from vicious razorback."

Kyle took the hand that was offered and stood on wobbly legs to face, or rather, look down on a strange-looking creature that barely came to his waist. Disproportionately long arms and big hands spoke of a life accustomed to swinging about in the trees, while big round eyes made it easier for the creature to see where it was going in the dark forest. The orange-yellow fur that covered all but the creature's face was wiry and smelled strongly of wood smoke.

"Thank you, Saffron. I owe you my life."

The creature smiled warmly. "Come. I take you to village. Others be there too."

She whirled around and began to move lithely along the narrow branch.

Kyle's legs remained firmly planted.

"What about my friend? We can't just leave without helping him."

Without pausing or looking back Saffron said, "Fat one fine. Others help him"

Kyle could still hear Lumpy laboring below but somehow he knew his friend would soon be in good hands. So, before Saffron could disappear into the darkness, he shuffled after her.

They moved along the branches, using the hanging vines to climb increasingly higher until the forest canopy became so dense they were able to walk along the flat, oval-shaped treetops. Above, the cavern shimmered like a star studded sky. Below, the forest was silent and dark. Ahead, a crackling fire welcomed them to the village on top of the world.

Megan saw Kyle coming and ran to greet him.

"What happened to Lumpy?" she mumbled. "Did that thing get him?"

Her mouth was so full her cheeks bulged. She could barely chew, let alone speak.

"I thought I heard him grumbling not too far behind me," said Kyle, dodging some spittle as it flew towards him and looking past Megan at a most remarkable scene.

The village Saffron had taken him to safety consisted of several dome-shaped huts that formed a concentric ring around a central fire pit. Shadowy figures no bigger than and just as hairy as Saffron wandered about, chattering noisily in small groups or sampling the various delicacies placed on trestle tables in the large open space between the fire pit and the huts. He noticed Ewewyrd and Freyja sitting alone in a dark corner, stuffing their faces and quietly enjoying each other's company. Distant points of light dotted the landscape, marking the location of other treetop villages.

Megan looked over Kyle's shoulder and groaned as Lumpy and his diminutive guide stepped out of the darkness surrounding the village. The guide had a spring to her step. Lumpy was bent forward with his head bowed, huffing and puffing and dragging his feet.

As Lumpy approached Megan and Kyle his head shot up and he suddenly became alert. Sniffing the air he said, loud enough for everyone in the village to hear, "I thought I smelled food."

"You better hurry," said Megan, popping a plump puffball in her mouth and sucking the juice from her fingers, "or there won't be anything left."

Lumpy's jaw dropped.

"What?"

Not wanting to lose out on all that good food Lumpy rushed away, charging full speed at a mass of bodies gathered around one of the tables. Someone saw him coming and warned the others, and the crowd scattered screaming just as he arrived.

"Friend very hungry," observed Saffron.

"Friend always hungry," said Megan.

Saffron giggled.

"Saffron and Burgundy go eat, too, before food really all gone." She took her companion's hand and strode away, leaving Kyle and Megan to fend for themselves.

"They certainly are friendly, trusting little creatures," said Kyle.

"Do you notice anything odd about them?" questioned Megan.

Kyle studied Saffron and the other villagers. "Only that they're all about the same size and covered in hair."

Megan clicked her tongue. "That's obvious. Take a closer look and tell me what else you see?"

He squinted to draw in the light and observe the pleasant scene more closely.

"The only other thing I see is Lumpy stuffing his fat face."

"Forget about that!"

"How can I? I'm starving."

Megan sighed. "Is that all you two ever think about? Food! Can't you see they're all girls?"

"So, what's wrong with that?"

"Don't you find that just a little bit odd?"

"The only thing I find odd is that I'm standing here talking to you while I could be over there stuffing my face." He eyed some remnants of the mushroom hanging from the corners of her mouth. "I see you've already helped yourself," he added, before leaving her to scrape away the remnants and pop them in her mouth.

Luckily, there was plenty of food to go around so Kyle found himself sampling everything, then going back and making a meal out of his favorites. While he and his companions chomped on their second hearty meal of the day, Saffron and Burgundy kept them company. Among other things, they learned that the strange little creatures were forest nymphs who are as much at home in the trees as humans and elves are on the ground. The nymphs also solved the mystery of day and night by using their high perch to point out the distant lava pits and explain how the molten rock rose and fell during the course of the day, much like the constant ebb and flow of the sea. When the lava was on the rise and at its highest point its radiant energy rebounded off the extremely reflective rock crystals embedded in the roof of the cavern, illuminating the underground world.

Before retiring for the evening the nymphs agreed to guide Kyle and his companions to the edge of the forest on the morrow, as close to Krungnir's Pass as the trees would take them. As Kyle lay under the crystal studded roof of the cavern he felt a tingling sensation run down both arms and wondered what tomorrow would bring.

KRUNGNIR'S PASS 10

THE MAGMA ROSE to the surface of the sprawling lava pits in a fiery
sea of orange, boiling over in bubbling waves and spilling onto the
charred wasteland between the Black Forest and the towering cliffs
that stretched east to west, in a manner of speaking, for as far as the
eye could see. As the molten rock filled the cavern with light, treetop
communities popped up everywhere, connected by rope bridges in
what amounted to an unbroken chain of wood-based islands in the
sky. Kyle looked beyond the living archipelago at the yawning gap that
was Krungnir's Pass, standing out like a deep black scar in the nearly
impervious wall of rock. It was going to be another very long day he
thought. He rubbed his face tiredly.

As soon as he touched his face he knew something was wrong
because his hands had never felt so strange and, while he really didn't
want to look at them, he was curious to see just how far the corruption
had spread. He wished he hadn't been so curious because when he
lowered his hands away from his face he was sickened by what he saw.
The flicker of hope that arrived on the heels of a new day fizzled and
burned out, to be replaced by a pained dismay.

Distracted by his grief, Kyle failed to hear Megan approach until it was too late.

"Does it hurt?" she said, gasping in his ear and staring in horror at his disfigured hands.

Kyle was positive that Megan and the others were fast asleep when he rose earlier and tiptoed away, but obviously he was mistaken. He quickly buried his hands in the folds of his cloak to hide them from her steady gaze.

"Only when I think about," he said. A shadow crossed his face, but he shook off the gloominess before it could take hold of him. "Which isn't very often."

Megan had her doubts. From the hurt in Kyle's eyes she was certain he was lying. She thought of taking pity on him, but there was no room in her heart to do so. Not when she knew that everything bad that had happened was his fault, and his fault alone.

"You could have made it easier for yourself – for all of us if the truth be told – if you weren't so darn stubborn," she said, regarding him critically.

He laughed mirthlessly.

"How?"

"By telling the king the reason you acted the way you did. I'm sure if he knew why you needed Draupner he would have been more understanding. He may have even offered to help you."

He rounded on her angrily.

"I tried to tell him but every time I opened my mouth that lout, Loki, jabbed me in the back with his sword. Besides, I doubt he would have listened to me."

"You should have done more to make him listen," Megan snapped back. "If not for us, then surely for your father's sake."

Tears glistened in his eyes. He knew Megan was right. He should have done more to plead his case when he had the chance. But it was too late now to mull over things he should have done. He turned away from Megan, too disheartened to respond.

●　　　　●　　　　●　　　　●

Jan tossed and turned in her sleep, struggling to shake off the demons that refused to let her rest in peace. "Leave me alone!" she said. "Leave me...!" She awoke with a start when a dark, shapeless hand appeared out of nowhere and fell across her face. Damp with sweat she sat up, shaking and gasping for air.

The bed sheets slipped through her sweaty palms and she shivered as her clammy skin met the cold damp air. It took her a moment to stop trembling, and by then, the queen had entered carrying a serving tray. The tray held a steaming wooden bowl.

"Good morning," chirped the queen. "I brought you something nice and warm that I hope will put some color back in your face."

She placed the tray on the bedside table, brushing aside a candle holder that got in the way. The holder and a clump of wax thumped unnoticed onto the floor.

"I do hope you are hungry," she added, observing for the first time the tormented look on Jan's face. "I'd hate to think that I carried this heavy tray all this way for nothing."

Jan sat up smartly to ease the queen's mind and to shake off the memories that still haunted her.

"I'm famished."

"Good. That must mean you're feeling better."

"Much better," Jan said, hiding her true feelings behind a buoyant smile.

The queen eyed her charge fondly "You'll feel even better once you've tried some of this."

She dipped a spoon in the steaming bowl, swirled the contents, scooped out a generous portion and proceeded to slake Jan's hunger.

●　　　　●　　　　●　　　　●

Just as promised, Saffron and Burgundy escorted Kyle and his companions to the edge of the Black Forest. Along the way they passed through several treetop villages and, much to their delight, they were greeted warmly by everyone they met. The affable nymphs showered them with food and anything that wasn't consumed immediately was loaded into packs which became increasingly bulky. The packs became so heavy, in fact, that they soon realized it was better to graciously decline further handouts than to have to lug around the extra weight. But that didn't stop Lumpy from stuffing his pack until it was so full he could barely close the flap.

While most of the villagers wished them well and merely saw them on their way, some of the younger, more curious nymphs tagged along to form what became a long, animated procession. At one point a few chords were struck on an instrument resembling a lute, setting off a chain reaction that culminated in well over a hundred melodic voices singing together as one. The merriment and music continued without pause until it was time to say good-bye.

It was a sad farewell for everyone, especially Megan. Not only had she grown fond of the nymphs, but she had the uncanny feeling that something terrible was going to happen. However, by the look of determination on Kyle's face and the sense of urgency in his step as they put the shadow of the Black Forest behind them, she realized it was time to move on. Resigned to this fact, she looked back with fondness at the crowd gathered on the treetops and waved until she could no longer hold her hand in the air. Finally, when it was virtually impossible to distinguish one diminutive figure from another, she turned her back on the distant cheers and wiped her hand across misty eyes, setting her sights on the daunting cliffs in the foreground.

•　　　•　　　•　　　•

Krungnir's Pass was a crack of land, not much wider than a cart path and strewn with boulders of all shapes and sizes. If you looked close enough at the sheer cliffs on either side of the rift you could see where some of the boulders had broken off, leaving behind ugly, jagged scars. Fortunately, Kyle and his companions approached on foot because it would have been almost impossible to navigate a cart or even a horse through the narrow, rock-strewn gap.

After pausing to rest and satisfy their hunger, they pressed on. However, no sooner had they set out than it became apparent that the passage was going to be a challenge. Not only did they have to maneuver through all the debris, but they had to constantly be on the lookout for falling rocks. Some of the missiles that rained down on them were the size of cannon balls, striking the ground with a boom and exploding on impact, sending forth dust clouds that hung in the air like smoke.

It was following one of these thunderous explosions that Kyle rounded a bend in the otherwise straight pass and, what he viewed through the hazy aftermath, made his heart skip a beat. His anguished moan was echoed by the others.

"Now what are we going to do?" said Megan, her eyes glued to a mountain of fallen rocks blocking the pass.

Once he got over the initial shock, Kyle saw the rock pile for what it really was; just another annoying obstacle they had to somehow overcome.

"The only thing we can do," said Kyle with more confidence than he felt. "We go over it."

Megan stared at him open-mouthed.

"Are you serious? Take a look! Those rocks are stacked together like a house of cards. One wrong move and the entire heap will come crashing down on whoever is dumb enough to go near it."

"I'm willing to give it a try," said Lumpy, stepping forward.

Kyle grabbed hold of the pack slung over Lumpy's right shoulder, stopping him dead in his tracks.

"I'll go first. It's my fault we're here in the first place. And, more importantly, I'm a lot lighter than you." He pushed past Lumpy. "You can follow me if I make it."

"You mean, when you make it," corrected Lumpy.

Kyle gave him a wan smile and moved towards the jumble of rocks. Meanwhile, Megan, Ewewyrd and Freyja crept backwards.

The earth at the base of the rock pile crunched beneath Kyle's feet, sending shivers down his spine as he imaged what his carcass would look like if the mountain was to come crashing down on him, crushing every bone in his body. Dispelling this idea, he hauled himself onto a sturdy-looking boulder that jutted out at the bottom, and used the smooth, flat surface as a foothold to begin his ascent.

Megan and Freyja shrieked when the first rock he reached for shifted, dislodging some of the smaller stones above it. He ducked beneath an overhanging boulder to avoid being pelted by the falling debris.

"I don't think this is such a good idea," said Megan, nervously eyeing the rock pile.

Kyle either failed to hear her or refused to listen. His heart beating wildly, he reached up and tested another rock. When nothing else rained down on him he gripped the rock and scrabbled up the side of the mountain, painfully slow at first, then more rapidly as he began to gain confidence. The higher he climbed, the more confident he became. Unfortunately, he also became more careless, and in his haste he lost his footing halfway up and slipped.

His heart thudded deafeningly in his ears, muffling the screams that pierced the uneasy silence. To slow his descent, he kicked and clawed at the surface of the rock pile, dislodging even more stones but eventually managing to cling onto something solid; a substantial boulder firmly wedged in place. The loose rocks clattered down the side of the mountain.

As he held on for his life he could feel the surface he was resting on slide out from under him, and he knew he was doomed when the boulder he was holding onto wiggled free and slowly edged downward. He tried to clamber over the rock but it was like swimming upstream against the current. The rock kept slipping further and further until, all of a sudden, it shot past him, sweeping him away and taking a sizeable piece of the mountain with it.

Lumpy watched in stunned silence as tons of bone crushing rock rumbled down the side of the mountain. The noise was so loud he had to cover his ears. That could have been me he told himself when he saw Kyle fall through the air and land heavily at the bottom, vanishing behind a cloud of dust. A wave of panic fluttered through his stomach. Feeling nauseous, he had to swallow hard to keep the bile from rising in his throat.

The rockslide was over almost as soon as it began and, even before the dust had settled, Lumpy and the others scrambled over to Kyle's limp body.

"Are you alright?" said Lumpy anxiously.

Kyle groaned and opened his eyes. He gazed bleary-eyed at Lumpy.

"I guess I should have let you go first," he said cracking a weak smile.

"I do have a lot more padding to cushion the fall."

Tears welled up in Megan's eyes.

"Is there anything we can do for you?"

She ran her eyes over Kyle but she didn't see any outward sign of injury; no river of blood or protruding, shattered bones.

Kyle regarded her strangely.

"You can help me up. These rocks are killing my back."

"But I thought..." She paused in mid-sentence, staring in awe at the rockslide and wondering how he could have survived without so much as a scratch.

"You thought I was a goner," said Kyle to finish what Megan began to say. "So did I but, luckily, most of the rocks came down ahead of me or I never would have made it."

He raised an arm and Lumpy assisted him to his feet. He made a face when he reached back to reposition his pack.

"It also helped that I was wearing this," he added, removing the pack generously provided by the nymphs and tipping it upside down. Along with some clumps of food that spilled to the ground, a gooey mess oozed out and plopped at his feet. He discarded the empty pack.

A few stray rocks rolled down the precipitous slope and clattered to the ground around them.

Ewewyrd circled restlessly.

"Let's get out of here before the rest of those rocks come down on us."

"Good idea," said Kyle. "I may not be so lucky the next time."

He moved away, limping slightly as he went. The others were so eager to distance themselves from the falling rocks that they failed to notice.

Once they were out of the danger zone Kyle paused and pulled out the map. He rubbed his chin thoughtfully as he unfolded it and scrutinized the rough sketch. The others huddled around him, wondering what he was thinking.

"What's on your mind?" Lumpy finally asked.

Kyle tapped the map with his forefinger, pointing to a dark, semi-circular mark at the base of the cliff.

"Do you know what this is?" he asked Ewewyrd.

Ewewyrd stared at the map.

"It looks like a cave."

"You're not sure?" said Megan.

"How could I be?" Ewewyrd barked back. "I've never been anywhere near there. Or weren't you listening to me the other day?"

Freyja placed a calming hand on Ewewyrd's shoulder.

"That's okay Ewewyrd. I know what it is."

"You do?" said Ewewyrd disbelievingly.

"Sure. You hear a lot of things you're not supposed to hear when you serve the head table." She sniggered as something humorous came to mind. "That's the entrance to the silk mines."

She saw that she had everyone's attention and this seemed to encourage her to continue. But before she did she turned to Megan and made a funny face.

"That's what the fine garments the king and queen always parade around in are made out of—silk." She tugged on the bottom of her ragged, sackcloth gown and pranced around like royalty. The threadbare material began to unravel in her hands so she had to release the disintegrating robe prematurely.

"I often hear them grumbling about the outrageous price the gnomes, who live in a village on the other side of the cliff, charge for their silk, and more than once I heard them talk about raiding the village. But rumor has it that the entrance to the cave is heavily guarded, so it's not that easy to gain access to the mines."

"But it is possible?" said Kyle.

"I suppose anything is possible," said Freyja.

"That's good enough for me."

Hopeful that there was still another way to reach their objective, Kyle refolded the map and secreted it away inside his cloak. Then, he hastened to retrace their steps and beat the ticking clock.

11
THE SILK MINES OF ARACH

DARKNESS FELL SOONER than expected and it wasn't until early the next morning that they reached the entrance to the silk mines. They came upon it suddenly, in the middle of nowhere, it seemed, standing out like an abscess in a mouthful of otherwise perfect teeth. If ever a cavity was welcome, this was one.

To be footsore and weary like the others was one thing, but to be in agony, too, was another. Yet, that's exactly how Kyle felt after the long trek. While the others may have thought something other than the curse was bothering him, they had no way of knowing for sure, beyond what he kept telling them, that the injury to his leg was more serious than first thought. He knew now, from stroking his thigh, that his pant leg was wet and sticky to the touch. It was only a good thing the cloak was long enough to cover up the bloody mess. It would have dampened waning spirits even further if they could see for themselves just how grave the wound actually was. So, as his limp became more and more pronounced and their concern for him grew, he managed to shrug off their worries by hiding behind a brave face and blatantly lying about how much his leg really hurt. He was glad when they came upon the entrance because they finally had something else to think about.

Freyja's assertion that the entrance was guarded was readily confirmed. On either side of a massive boulder that blocked the access an enormous troll stood guard, immobilized by a thick neck restraint fastened to a heavy chain. The chains, which were fed through two holes on either side and in the base of a guard tower constructed overtop of the huge boulder, could be loosened or tightened by turning the crank on a pair of winches bolted to the tower. At the moment, the chains were taut, giving the trolls very little freedom of movement. Ankle and wrist fetters restricted the beasts further.

"What do you want?" said a gaunt, craggy-faced gnome with beady, blood-shot eyes.

He glared at them from his perch atop the guard tower, his bulbous, vein-streaked nose glistening like a beacon.

At the sound of the gnome's gravelly voice the trolls became agitated, choking and hacking like a pair of unruly mastiffs tugging on their leashes. Kyle and the others stepped back wisely, distancing themselves from the slobbering beasts.

"Well?" the gnome growled.

He took a long draught from a wineskin resting on his bony hip.

Kyle cleared his throat.

"To get to the other side," he said, gazing longingly at the wineskin and licking his parched lips.

The gnome spat, spraying one of the trolls. The unruly beast snarled at him.

"Are you crazy? No one is allowed to enter without permission."

Megan glanced around hopefully.

"Is there anyone around we can talk to get permission? You see, we really need to get to the other side."

The gnome frowned so hard his eyes nearly disappeared in the folds of loose skin on his face.

"The only one here is me," he said harshly. He took another swig from the wineskin and belched contentedly.

"In that case, good sir," purred Megan, "we'd like your permission to enter." She masked her disdain behind a disarming smile.

The gnome's scowl deepened and, for a moment, it looked as if he was going to refuse. Then something clicked and he almost cracked a smile as his glazed eyes homed in on the food pack slung over Megan's shoulders. He rubbed his bristly chin, lifting the wineskin and squeezing out a mouthful.

"Suppose I say yes," he slurred. "What's in it for me?"

Reading the gnome's mind, Megan removed the pack and dropped it on the ground in front of her. Reaching inside, she dug around until she came up with something she knew would spark his interest. His eyes lit up as she removed her hand and presented him with an exceptionally large puffball.

"And there's another one inside just like it," she said, tossing the puffball up to the gnome.

He stuffed the mushroom in his mouth.

"What else?" he spat.

Freyja and Ewewyrd stepped forward and set their packs next to Megan's. While Freyja removed a handful of colorful berries, Ewewyrd withdrew a mushroom loaf that had one or two nibbles at either end.

The gnome pointed a wine stained finger at Lumpy.

"What about you?"

Lumpy snorted.

"You can't have everything, you greedy little thief. What are we going to eat?"

"That's your problem, not mine."

The wineskin spluttered as the gnome attempted to squeeze out the last of the cloudy liquid.

All eyes were on Lumpy as they waited to see what he would do. Even the trolls ceased tugging on their tethers and viewed the fat human with interest.

"You already been offered more than enough," said Lumpy with a contemptuous look. "Take it or leave it."

He crossed his arms in a huff, determined not to bend.

Disappointed that the wineskin was empty, the gnome tossed it aside and returned Lumpy's venomous look.

"It's all or nothing. The choice is yours."

Megan released a heavy sigh.

"For heaven's sake, Hector, give him what he wants and stop wasting time bickering over a few scraps of food."

She reached for the pack but Lumpy swung it away from her grasping hands.

"It's Lumpy, you stupid girl! And I won't give that drunken gnome all the food we've got."

"Have it your way," the gnome said, licking his fingers and smacking his lips. "You must not be that desperate to get to the other side, in spite of what the 'stupid girl' said."

Lumpy couldn't help but notice the exasperated look on Kyle's face and, as much as it pained him to hand over the last of their supplies, he knew he had no choice. Muttering under his breath, he ripped the pack off his back and tossed it beside the others.

"I hope you choke on it."

The gnome regarded the four bulging packs with predatory eyes.

"Better me, than you," he said, reaching across to release the catch on one of the winches and slowly letting out the chain.

Amazingly, the troll stopped struggling and chose to move purposefully towards the boulder as the chain was gradually released in stages. Once the boulder was within reach the beast leaned into it, let out a terrifying roar and pushed with all its might. At first nothing happened, but then the rock groaned and moved slightly. The troll saw this and it pushed even harder, roaring louder and thrusting upwards with its powerful legs until the boulder started to roll along a timeworn groove in the ground. Sweat poured down its sinewy back and arms, dripping in puddles at its feet. Throughout it all, the other troll became more and more agitated.

As soon as the boulder was rolled clear of the entrance the troll paused to catch its breath. With its chest still heaving from exertion, the beast lumbered back to claim the leg of lamb the gnome had tossed on the ground, not too far from the spot it had been chained to earlier. The gnome turned the crank, frantically reeling in the chain while the troll chomped noisily on the leg.

"Hurry," the gnome said. "It won't be long before it finishes that and is looking around for something else to devour."

"But it is pitch-black in there," said Megan. "How do you expect us to see where we're going?"

It just so happened that there was a pitch covered torch within reach on the guard tower, so the gnome snatched it, held it over a blazing brazier until it ignited and tossed it into the cave.

"There. Now hurry up. And don't forget my goodies. You can leave them on the ground just inside the cave. I'll be down to get them later."

Kyle hobbled past the preoccupied troll, entering the cave and reaching down for the torch. He heard three packs hit the ground behind him as Megan, Ewewyrd and Freyja zoomed past him. Then finally, he heard the last pack and he felt Lumpy's hot breath on the back of his neck.

No sooner had they stepped inside the cave when the ground shook and the boulder rumbled across the entrance. As near darkness set in Lumpy ogled the packs.

"Don't even think of it," said the gnome, aiming a spear at Lumpy from a platform that extended inside the cave and gave the guard access to the tower without ever having to go outside. The extension was supported by a large crossbeam fixed to two wooden posts. A rope ladder, rolled up next to the gnome, showed how he got up and down.

Kyle placed a hand on Lumpy's shoulder.

"Come on, Lumpy. We can always find something else to eat later."

Lumpy shook his fist at the inhospitable gnome.

"Like I said—I hope you choke on it."

He allowed himself to be led away but not before booting his pack and scattering much of the contents.

The gnome smiled grimly at the shadowy figures. "You'll find something alright," he said in a low, sinister voice that suddenly sounded sober, "but it won't be to your liking." He cackled wickedly.

The gnome's laughter filled the air with a spectral echo that sent shivers down their spine. They huddled around the torchlight.

•   •   •   •

Lumpy was still fuming much later when they came upon the heart of the tunnel. It was at this point they found themselves looking at a series of narrow, secondary passages on either side. As they shuffled past the first dark opening the air thickened with an aroma so vile it made them gag.

"What's that awful smell?" Megan said, her voice muffled by the hand cupped over her mouth, pinching her nose.

"Don't look at me," said Lumpy in defensive. "Even I don't smell that bad."

Megan frowned at him.

"Well, I don't," insisted Lumpy.

In the silence that followed, a murmuring scuffling sound arose like waves washing over a pebbly beach. Kyle poked the torch into one of the passages and he saw something stir, withdrawing to the absolute darkness beyond the flickering glow. He stepped inside to get a closer look but was blinded momentarily by a flash of light. Sparks rained down on him as a web spun across the opening sizzled and disintegrated from the intense heat.

He was about to back away when a loud rip split the air and something of considerable bulk tore through a cocoon-like mass of spider silk blanketing the wall of the passage. He waved the torch to see what it was.

Waves of horror flooded through him as he gaped at the desiccated remains of an unfortunate soul who must have stumbled upon the web. The corpse, which appeared to be the same size and shape as Ewewyrd, leaned forward at an awkward angle, its skeletal face grimacing menacingly. A gaping wound in the victim's stomach was crawling with pus-colored maggots.

Pity turned to panic when he noticed a huge, shapeless figure, obscured by the gloom, slowly shuffling towards him. He backed up suddenly, bumping into something. He could tell by the stale breath that it was Lumpy.

"Get out of here!" he said, his voice trembling with fear.

Once again Kyle tried to back out of the passage and, once again, Lumpy stood in his way. Frustrated, he rounded on his friend in anger.

"Didn't you hear me, you moron? Move!"

He tried to force Lumpy to move, shoving him in the chest, but he failed miserably.

Normally, Lumpy would have been annoyed, at Kyle or anyone else who dared to push him around, but when he saw the look of terror in Kyle's eyes his anger dissolved.

"What's did you see?" he asked.

"Nothing."

"Nothing!" said an incredulous Lumpy. "What do you think I am? A fool."

He stood on the tips of his toes and peered over Kyle's shoulder, but it was too dark to really see anything.

Kyle placed a restraining hand on Lumpy's shoulder, bringing him down to eye level. "We have to get out of here now," he said through gritted teeth.

His curiosity aroused, Lumpy had no intention of leaving until he got a better look at the thing that frightened Kyle. Fortunately, he didn't have long to wait. He was still trying to penetrate the darkness when an ear-piercing scream made him step back out of the passage; something Kyle had wanted him to do all along.

"Something touched me," said Freyja.

Kyle's heart skipped a beat when he swung the torch around and saw a gigantic spider standing over Freyja, poised to strike. As the creature's long, wicked jaws descended, he thrust the torch in its ugly face. The spider let out an anguished squeal and scurried away, dragging its round, bloated body along the floor of the passage. Muted sounds arose all around them as more of the creatures moved stealthily into position.

Freyja let out another scream. Only this time Megan and Ewewyrd joined in too.

"They're everywhere," cried Megan.

Kyle waved the torch around wildly, trying to see where the next attack would come from. He observed several dark blobs vanish like a flash into the tunnels up ahead.

"Follow me," he said, brandishing the torch like a flaming sword, "and stay close."

They moved forward with caution, and each time they came to a tunnel Kyle lashed out and stabbed at the gleaming red eyes hovering near the opening. The startled creatures screeched as they were either singed by the initial thrust or engulfed in flames when the highly flammable webs caught fire. Soon the air around them was rank with the smell of burning flesh.

A few minutes later they came upon the last passage and, as they shuffled safely past it, they were filled with hope by a sliver of natural light shining faintly in the distance. Throwing caution to the wind, they made a mad dash for what they thought would be an easy exit, leading directly to Arach. Instead, they found themselves staring at another massive boulder. Only this time they were standing on the wrong side of the obstacle. And they could hear the overgrown arachnids coming for them, their bloated bodies scraping along the ground.

Kyle came to the sudden realization that the entrance wasn't blocked to keep intruders out of the silk mines but to keep the spiders in, where the webs they spun provided the raw material for the lucrative silk industry. He looked upon this revelation with the same sense of doom as anyone else who might have faced the fangs of death that were now bearing down on them.

"What do we do now?" Megan asked, her ashen face breaking out in a cold sweat.

Under the circumstances, they really only had one option; escape or be devoured. Kyle regarded the narrow gap above the sphere-shaped boulder and considered the chances of scaling the framework that supported the access platform and taking the lookout by surprise. From the sounds of loud snoring coming from the guard tower he thought the chances were good. Turning to Ewewyrd, he whispered something in the elf's ear.

Ewewyrd reached inside the pouch strapped around his waist and removed a handful of fairy dust, which he promptly sprinkled over himself. The glittering dust rained down on him and before the last speck hit the ground he vanished.

The guard tower creaked but not enough to rouse the sleeping guard. The snores continued unabated.

"Hurry!" whispered Kyle. "I don't know how long I can hold them off."

He whirled round to face the oncoming spiders. Meanwhile, Lumpy, Megan and Freyja ducked behind him and cowered in fear.

Kyle waved the torch fiercely, keeping the screeching spiders at bay. Through the din of battle he heard a chain rattle and a startled cry, but he was too busy to think anything of it. His heart skipped a beat when the flame fluttered. Sensing that the torch was about to expire, the spiders retreated slightly, biding their time away from the scorching heat.

A moment before the torch sputtered and died the ground rumbled beneath their feet and the boulder trembled to life. As it rolled across the opening, Lumpy heard a startled shriek and saw a body plunge to the ground through the hole that had opened up. The troll leaning into the boulder abandoned its post to claim the gift that had fallen from the sky.

"Let's get out of here while we have the chance," said Lumpy, putting a hand on Megan and Freyja and heaving them through the narrow opening. All three of them sprinted past the troll to the sound of cracking bones and tearing flesh.

As soon as the torch expired Kyle tossed it at the hoard, striking the first spider bold enough to rush at him in the head and creating some confusion. While the creature squealed and stumbled about in pain, and the other spiders scrambled to get out of its way, Kyle slipped through the opening and hobbled past the trolls.

"Where's Ewewyrd?" he said, limping up to Lumpy, Megan and Freyja, his face contorted in pain.

"I'm right behind you," panted Ewewyrd.

Kyle looked back but all he could see were the two trolls fighting over the bloody remains of the guard, and the giant spiders spilling out of the cave. He felt a gust of air and he knew that Ewewyrd had just streaked past them.

"Where to now?" asked Lumpy, glancing around at the orderly scene below.

They stood on a rise above Arach, looking down at the bustling merchant town nestled on the edge of an expansive sea. Initially, Kyle had intended to skirt around the town but, given their current predicament, that plan would have to be altered. With the spiders stampeding down the hill after them, Kyle set his sights on the busy wharf, scrutinizing each vessel until he saw exactly what he was looking for—a skiff. At the moment two squat figures were busy unloading the small rowboat and, like everyone around them, they were oblivious to the danger heading their way.

"Change of plans," said Kyle, in response to Lumpy's question. "You see that skiff down there?"

Lumpy followed the line of his outstretched black finger.

"You mean that rowboat? What about it?"

"That's our ticket to freedom."

The spiders were so close now Lumpy could make out their gleaming red eyes. "Then what are we waiting for? Let's go for it."

Before anyone could disagree, he turned and fled. The others followed close on his heels.

They sprinted down the hill, bursting onto a crowded street with portable stalls squeezed tightly together on either side. Shouts of indignation were followed by shrieks of terror and cries of pain as Kyle and his companions cut a trail through the crowd and the ravenous spiders followed in their wake.

While the spiders gorged themselves on gnome, Kyle and the others kept up the torrid pace until they reached the skiff. Lumpy ploughed into the first boatman and heaved him in the water before he knew what hit him. The backsplash rained down on Ewewyrd, washing away the fairy dust and revealing him bent over unlashing the stern rope. The second boatman was waiting for Lumpy when he leaped onto the skiff. He managed to put up a good fight, but only until Megan picked up one of the oars and pushed him overboard. She jumped into the boat, along with Ewewyrd and Freyja. Kyle unlashed the bow rope and joined the others just as a lone spider came charging towards them.

Lumpy plopped down between the oars and started rowing for his life.

"Faster!" screamed Megan. "Faster!"

"I'm going as fast as I can," wheezed Lumpy.

The oars chopped at the surface, splashing water everywhere as the rowboat moved away from the wharf agonizingly slow.

Ewewyrd and Freyja leaned over the side of the boat and began paddling with their hands. Megan trembled and gnawed on her fingernails. Kyle sat in the bow, grimacing in pain and gripping his throbbing leg.

The spider saw the skiff pulling out to sea and sped up. As it reached the end of the wharf, it hurled its massive body in the air, hitting the water next to the boat with a splat and soaking everyone on board. It briefly bobbed up and down like a buoy, then it sank like a rock; its eight stubby legs flailing fruitlessly as it descended.

Relieved that the danger had passed, Lumpy relaxed his grip on the oars. Eventually he forgot about their most recent brush with death and the scene of utter chaos that led to a swift departure from Arach, and he turned his thoughts to more important things; like where their next meal was going to come from now that they gave all their food to that underhanded gnome.

12
JOTUNHEIM

THE SKIFF GLIDED across the surface of the water, barely causing a ripple in the endless, shimmering sea. While the others slept soundly, Lumpy passed the time splashing the oars lazily in the water and scoffing down the contents of a keg he found rolling around in the boat. The amber liquid went down smoothly, washing away the dust clinging to the back of his throat and warming his insides. Before long his eyelids grew heavy so he pulled in the oars and leaned back, drawing comfort from the sweet nectar and the serene stillness of the water. Extending his legs and yawning, he closed his eyes and allowed the gently rocking boat to lull him to sleep.

They drifted aimlessly until the sound of water lapping on a nearby shore woke Kyle from his slumber. He shivered as a cool, damp breeze found its way inside his cloak and chilled him to the bone. Through sleepy eyes he saw phantom shapes looming in the mist carried by a gentle breeze.

"Land ho," he said, rousing the others.

Lumpy dipped the oars in the water and steered the skiff towards a narrow channel between two desolate, wind-swept islands. His target was a sprawling coastline, dotted with mushroom-shaped trees on the other side of the strait.

Megan's face lit up for a moment when she caught a glimpse of the peculiar shaped trees. Despite the feeling of doom that swept over her when she first entered the Black Forest, she had nothing but fond memories when she thought of the lovable nymphs who dwelled among its treetops. As the boat approached the channel she gazed intently at the distant trees, scanning the canopy for signs of life, but there were no nymph-like beings to be seen; or any other living creatures for that matter.

Upon entering the narrow strait the winds began to pick up, and the calm sea suddenly became restless. As the air howled and swirled around them, the agitated waves slapped against the boat, whipping the chilly dampness over the sides and tossing the vessel about. It gave a lurch and the sea rushed in.

Megan, Ewewyrd and Freyja grabbed whatever was at hand and began bailing yet, no sooner had they tossed the water overboard than the boat rode a crest and more of the wretched stuff poured in, flooding the aft section.

"Turn around!" Kyle shouted, seconds before the bow was swallowed up by a huge wave and he disappeared behind a curtain of water.

"I'm trying to but I can't," said Lumpy, chopping at the frothing sea.

Kyle reappeared as the bow rose out of the murky depths.

"What?"

"I can't," repeated Lumpy.

He pulled on the oars but nothing happened. The boat merely rocked back and forth, refusing to budge.

"Why? What's stopping you?"

Lumpy stared at Kyle open-mouthed.

"I don't know. You tell me."

Perplexed, Kyle peered over the side of the vessel, and through the swelling waves, he saw a dark, hulking mass just below the surface. At first he thought the boat had been heaved up onto a reef or a rocky ridge between the two islands, and was in grave danger of being scuttled. But then he saw the dark mass thrash back and forth, stirring up the water and sending forth more waves. It glided under the boat and disappeared.

Kyle recoiled, uttering an audible gasp.

Sensing his fear, the others held their breath, anticipating a horror only they could imagine. But even though they conjured up the most dreadful images conceivable, they weren't prepared for what they saw. A wave of panic swept over them, as easily as the sea rushed over the sides of the boat, when an enormous, eel-like creature broke through the surface in a plume of foaming water and menacing, jagged teeth, jarring loose the oar on the starboard side and hurling it into the air.

Megan, Ewewyrd and Freyja screamed in unison and instinctively wrapped their arms around each other for protection. Meanwhile, Lumpy splashed at the water with one oar and Kyle dove to catch the other one before it plunged into the sea.

The serpent reared up out of the water and prepared to strike, venom dripping from its fearsome fangs and hissing as it splashed into the sea. After what seemed like an eternity, the creature lashed out at the threesome crowded together at the back of the boat.

With no regard for his own safety, Kyle lunged forward and thrust the oar between the serpent's gaping jaws. The oar shattered like a toothpick as the jaws snapped shut a hair from Megan's face.

The serpent roared, tossing aside the splintered wood with a violent shake of its massive reptilian head. Then it struck again, only this time Lumpy stood up and swung the other oar around, cracking it off the side of the creature's thick, scaly skull.

Screeching in anger, the serpent whipped its head around, knocking the oar out of Lumpy's hand and fixing him with its evil eyes. The crocodilian mouth curled up in a grim smile.

Lumpy found himself frozen by fear, an easy target for the vengeful serpent's fury. He closed his eyes so he didn't have to bear witness to his own demise.

As the creature's hot breath licked at his face Lumpy felt a tug on his shirt, but he still didn't move. He was transfixed by the serpent's gaze. Kyle pulled harder a second time and this time Lumpy stumbled backwards, tumbling over the oarsman's seat and rolling to safety just before the serpent hammered the seat, smashing it to smithereens and splitting some of the floorboards. Water seeped through the cracks.

The serpent plunged into the turbulent sea, vanishing behind a wall of water that shot upwards and outwards to slam into the boat and toss the occupants about like balls in a pinball machine.

Despite the confusion, Megan needed to have her wits about her as Ewewyrd and Freyja went screaming past her in opposite directions. The somersaults they performed were purely accidental and she had to move fast to snatch them out of midair before their momentum sent them reeling over the sides of the boat.

While Lumpy threw himself face down over the shattered floorboards, hoping to stop the sea from gushing in, Kyle watched Megan's heroics in stunned silence. He was horrified when he saw the elves roll up the sides of the boat and flip through the air, but thrilled by Megan's rapid response. The euphoria he felt was short-lived however when, through a fountain of bubbling, frothing water, the serpent's ugly maw reappeared. Its eyes glistened fiercely as it focused on the plump figure sprawled out face down in the middle of the boat, unable to offer any resistance.

Before delivering the death blow the serpent tilted its head back and roared, making the few hairs on Ewewyrd's head stand up and sending shivers down Megan and Freyja's spine. The trio watched in horror as venom poured from the creature's yawning mouth, splattering onto the boat with a burning, hissing sound and searing a hole in Lumpy's pants. He yelped and patted at his smoking backside.

With lightning speed the serpent struck at Lumpy but once again Kyle foiled it by plunging the broken oar through one of its gleaming eyes. As the creature shook its head madly and squealed in agony it caught Kyle with its fangs, ripping the cloak open and stabbing him in the shoulder. Megan caught a glimpse of Draupner and the blackened skin around Kyle's shoulder and chest, and gasped in horror at the extent of the putrefaction.

Kyle flew through the air, numbed senseless by the excruciating pain. The last thing he saw before he hit the water and went under was the serpent as it fell like a mighty oak, crashing down on the skiff. When he resurfaced the vile creature was nowhere in sight, and what remained of the boat spiraled downward while the sea gurgled around it. He heard the others shouting, calling out his name, but he couldn't see them through the dense fog. He tried to yell back, to let them know that he was still alive, only the pain was too intense. Instead, he gagged on a mouthful of water.

He felt the poison coursing through his body and he knew it was only a matter of time before he would begin convulsing and die a most agonizing death. Foreseeing that bitter moment, he slipped beneath the surface with the intention of taking matters into his own hands. Once again he found himself struggling to hold on to his last breath and in the depths of despair he came to the conclusion that it must have always been his destiny to drown in some obscure, godforsaken place. With the whole world swimming about him his lungs began to fill with water and he slowly lost consciousness.

Kyle was led to believe that death is a pleasant experience, so it came as no surprise when he heard angels singing and he felt himself floating effortlessly above the sea. What he didn't understand was why, if he was dead, his chest was burning and every muscle in his body ached. Even his eyelids stung as he struggled to pry them open.

Through half closed lids he saw Megan and Lumpy suspended in midair in front of him. Ahead of them but much higher were Ewewyrd and Freyja. Rather than soaring through the sky on wings of their own, all four of his companions were being guided along by a pair of winged goddesses, who gripped their charges firmly around the shoulder while hovering alongside them. Their humming wings were like music to his ears. He lowered his eyelids and drifted off, wondering who the angelic figures were and how much longer he would be able to cheat death.

• • • •

After wasting two days lying in bed fretting about every little thing that came to mind, Jan was ready for a change of scenery. So she was both delighted and relieved when the queen asked her if she felt well enough to accompany her on a stroll through the royal garden. Jan leapt at the opportunity; making the queen wonder if she hadn't put a little too much zing in that last batch of medicinal soup she had concocted for her patient.

Much to her surprise, the garden was a wonderful diversion, stimulating her senses with copious sights and smells and taking her mind off the disturbing thoughts that had haunted her day and night. Whoever designed the grounds knew exactly what they were doing because, although the plants and flowers lacked the vivid colors Jan was used to seeing in a typical garden, there was enough variety and contrast to make it interesting nonetheless. Every now and then the designer interjected a tasteful ornament to compliment a particular plant or a comfortable bench to persuade visitors to sit and stay a while.

One ornament in particular caught Jan's eye and caused a flood of memories. As she gazed at the cherubic statue, tears streamed down her cheeks and splashed in the tiny pool at the water boy's feet.

The queen, who had been nattering incessantly, noticed the tears and immediately felt guilty for rambling and not giving Jan a chance to say much of anything.

"What is it, my dear? Am I talking too much? I really must

apologize but it's not often I get to talk about my garden with someone who enjoys it as much as I do."

Jan's tears were as ceaseless as the queen's chatter.

"Please," said the queen, taking Jan gently by the shoulders and bending down to look her straight in the eyes. "Tell me what's troubling you."

"It's my parents," said Jan, blubbering and sniffling. Her eyes were red and swollen, and twin trails of mucus ran from her nose.

"You miss them. Don't you?"

"No—I mean, yes," said Jan, correcting herself. "Of course I miss them. I miss them dearly. But that's not why I'm so upset."

"What is it then?" pressed the queen, her voice ringing with concern.

Jan tried to relax by taking a deep breath. It seemed to help. The tears slowed to a trickle as she said, "Everything bad that has happened is because of my parents."

"Oh!" said the queen startled.

Jan noticed the confusion.

"It's not what you think," said Jan, struggling to contain the tears. "When Kyle took the ring—the one you call Draupner—he didn't take it for himself. He was thinking about my parents and what they could do with all that gold."

"I'm sure he was," said the queen severely. "Just like everyone else who has tried to get their hands on it. It's always for the benefit of someone else—or so they say. Why do you think we keep it secreted away behind these walls?" She waved her hand at the lofty barrier encircling the palace.

"No. That's not what I mean," wailed Jan behind a fresh flood of tears. "It's my daddy who needs it. You see, he has cancer, and unless we can come up with the money to pay for his treatments, he'll die."

"Cancer?" the queen said. She appeared even more perplexed. "I'm afraid I don't know what that is."

"It's this dreadful disease," said Jan snuffling. "My daddy has to go to the hospital a lot but it's very expensive, so mommy had to sell almost everything we own…even some of my toys…and now this mean old man with bad breath and greasy hair wants to take our house…and my mommy's boss keeps saying he's going to fire her unless she stops missing so much work…and Kyle was so happy when he found some coins, he thought for sure there was treasure in the cave but there wasn't any…then we ended up here…so he just had to take it."

Exhausted, she collapsed into the queen's outstretched arms and buried her tear-streaked face in the royal bosom.

The queen had been listening intently to everything Jan had to say and, as she read between the lines, a picture began to emerge that was altogether different than the one she had formulated in her mind. If Jan was telling the truth, and there was really no reason to doubt the child, then the ungrateful boy everyone took to be greedy and unselfish was anything but. She felt a pang of guilt for not doing more to help Kyle and the others. However, at the time, there was very little she could do—the king had already made up his mind.

"But why didn't Kyle say something? The king may be strict when he has to be but, deep down inside, he has a heart of gold. He would have never treated your brother so callously knowing what I know now."

"He was going to," sniffed Jan. "but every time he opened his mouth that brute, Loki, poked him with his sword."

"Oh, he did. Did he?" The queen was already thinking of ways to punish Loki.

Jan nodded dejectedly.

"Well, it's time the king got to hear the truth," the queen said, taking Jan by the hand and gently leading her away. "I only hope it's not too late."

•   •   •   •

Kyle woke with a start, sitting up suddenly and reaching for his leg. But the pain that jolted him awake was nothing compared to the explosion inside his head that quickly made him forget about the injured limb and the winged goddess leaning over him. Groaning, he clamped his hands to his head to see if he could stop the pounding and collapsed on the spongy turf.

"Don't make any sudden moves," the goddess said.

Now she tells me, Kyle thought to himself. He yelped when the goddess slapped a warm, damp clump of something that resembled greenish mud on his thigh, covering up a deep red gash. The skin near the gash and all down his bare leg was as black as the cloak, folded back to expose the injury he sustained when the rock pile had slipped out from under him. She smoothed out the clump with soft, graceful hands that mirrored the elegant lines of her vibrant, youthful face, and wrapped a strip of cloth around his throbbing thigh to hold the mudpack in place. Then, she repositioned the cloak to conceal his discolored leg from snooping eyes.

Within seconds the stinging in his leg was gone, and the relaxing, healing mud began to penetrate deeply, coursing through his body like a gentle breeze on a hot summer's day. Soon, muscles that had been aching for days no longer ached and, even though his brain seemed clouded by a thick fog, his head stopped pounding.

"Where am I?" he said weakly.

He was obsessed by the girl's beauty; her golden hair, deep blue eyes and the upward curvature of her full, red lips. So obsessed, in fact, he found it hard to take his eyes off her.

Her lips curled up in an engaging smile.

"Jotunheim."

Kyle's face drew a blank.

"Jotunheim?" he repeated.

"Realm of the giants," the goddess said in response to his vacant expression.

Kyle regarded her strangely.

"I always thought giants were bigger—" He paused, gazing intently at her enchanting face. "—and uglier."

"They are," she tittered, "much bigger and much uglier than us fairies." She blushed under his intense gaze.

Kyle felt the blood rushing to his cheeks as well and looked away to avoid further embarrassment. From the light peeking through the canopy overhead he knew they were surrounded by mushroom-shaped trees much like in the Black Forest, and a quick glance around revealed that they were in a glade in the woods. The sheltered clearing appeared peaceful and serene, unlike the patch of ground they so willingly surrendered to the rampaging razorback. He breathed a sigh of relief when he noticed Megan and Lumpy snoozing on the ground nearby.

His thoughts had turned to his other two companions when the sounds of laughter made him look the other way and he observed Ewewyrd warming himself by a blazing fire. The elf was talking animatedly to another fairy; the butterfly-like wings that protruded from her back fluttered gently back and forth, stirring up the occasional spark. While the two chatted like old friends, Freyja dipped a ladle into a cauldron suspended over the fire and scooped out some of the contents. Then she poured the liquid into a gourd bowl, danced around the sparks and headed in Kyle's direction.

Freyja greeted him with a warm smile.

"How's the patient doing?" she asked the fairy.

"As well as can be expected," the fairy said, before Kyle had a chance to speak.

As Freyja handed the bowl to the fairy, Kyle's nostrils were assailed by a foul odor.

"I hope you don't expect me to drink that," he said, making a face and casting a wary eye on the bowl.

"It's for your own good," said Freyja sternly. "Isn't that right, Idunn?"

So that's her name Kyle thought to himself. He liked it just as much as he liked to believe Idunn was a real goddess.

"I know it smells disgusting," said Idunn, dipping an elongated finger in the bowl and stirring the contents, "but it's just what your body needs. Especially after all that bezoar stone we had to pour down your throat. Normally, one dose of the antidote will do but you had so much of the serpent's poison in your blood we had to give you a second dose."

Kyle had no idea what Idunn was talking about. The last thing he remembered was watching the others being carried away by angels while he floated above a calm sea. Then he recalled feeling sleepy and closing his eyes. After that there was only darkness.

"I don't understand," he said. "When did all this happen?"

"Within minutes of the fairies plucking us from the sea," said Freyja. "I'm not surprised you don't remember. By the time we arrived here you were delirious."

Idunn slipped a hand behind Kyle's neck to prop him up.

"You must have thought I was your sister because you kept calling me Jan and asking about our father."

"You seemed genuinely concerned," added Freyja. "I do hope nothing is wrong with your father."

Fortunately, Idunn chose that moment to stick the steaming bowl in Kyle's face. He gagged as he took a sip of the malodorous brew and, when Idunn lowered the bowl to let him breathe, she attributed his watery eyes to the concoction's equally repellent taste. So did Freyja for that matter.

Idunn gave him a reassuring grin.

"I know it's strong but it has to be to dissolve any undigested bezoar stone. That stuff is almost as toxic as the serpent's poison if it sits in your stomach too long."

The next time Idunn raised the bowl Kyle was ready. He held his breath until the moment was right. Then, instead of prolonging the agony by taking little sips, he grasped the bowl, tilted his head back and downed the contents.

"Before today, my grandma's kidney bean pie was the worst thing I ever tasted," said Kyle, making a disgusting face and handing Idunn the empty bowl. "But this stuff makes that taste like candy."

Idunn and Freyja giggled.

"What did you do?" he added. "Wring out my socks and throw in the dirty water?"

Kyle wriggled his bare feet, coloring with the realization that he was only partially dressed.

Idunn noted the look of embarrassment on his face.

"Don't worry. Your friend Lumpy and Ewewyrd removed your clothes while my sisters and I prepared the antidote and the ointment I used to treat your wounds. By the way, how is your shoulder feeling?"

Kyle placed a hand on his shoulder, feeling a warm lump under the cloak. As he held his hand there he could almost feel the ointment at work, mending the torn flesh.

"It feels better already."

He tried to sit up on his own but fell back down after feeling slightly nauseous and light-headed.

"I'm glad to hear that," said Idunn, placing a restraining hand on his chest. "Now get some rest. You'll feel much better for it."

In light of all the time they had lost, Kyle didn't feel much like resting. So he tried to will himself to stand. But his muscles refused to respond. They seemed to be enjoying a much needed holiday compliments of Idunn's wonderful, healing ointment. Through sleepy eyes he saw Idunn and Freyja glide away and join several blurry figures huddled around the camp fire. Their murmuring voices drifted through the silent glade and lulled him to sleep within minutes.

He slept like a corpse for the rest of the day and well into the next morning realizing as he rose refreshed and glanced around the empty glade that Idunn and her sisters had slipped away in the dead of night.

Not that it came as much of a surprise. He recalled Ewewyrd telling him about the enigmatic fairies. How they lived like nomads, straying from place to place, never staying too long in one location. "That way they are always one step ahead of the relentless fairy hunters, who would go to any length to capture one of the magical beings," Ewewyrd had told him. The elf was probably the only outsider they trusted, having endeared himself to them years ago by freeing one of Idunn's sisters from a hunter's snare. It was probably this trust that saved Kyle's life. His heart went out to Idunn and her sisters, who he would probably never see again.

He noticed that someone had placed his dry clothes nearby and was in the process of getting dressed when a familiar scream cut through the air like a knife. "Now what?" he groaned, stepping into his shoes and wondering what Megan was screaming about now.

For a moment the forest was as silent as the grave. Then another, more desperate shriek split the air, followed by crashing through the undergrowth. Sensing the need to defend himself, Kyle looked around for something he could use as a weapon but there was nothing close at hand. He began to panic as the snapping branches and heavy breathing grew louder.

Dismayed, he was about to run for cover when Ewewyrd and Freyja rushed into the glade and startled him. They were both visibly shaken.

"They've captured Megan and Lumpy," said Ewewyrd panting heavily. His knees clacked together as he gazed wide-eyed at Kyle.

"Who did?" asked Kyle.

"The giants," said Freyja, placing a hand between Ewewyrd's knees to stop them from clacking. "We were in the forest foraging for food when we came across a cart path. I told him not to follow it but he wouldn't listen."

Kyle regarded Ewewyrd harshly.

"Not me," said Ewewyrd. "Lumpy."

"Anyhow," continued Freyja. "As soon as we rounded the first corner there they were. Over a dozen of them mounted and armed to the teeth. They must have stopped after they heard us arguing." A feeling of guilt swept through her veins. She looked away so Kyle didn't see the hurt in her eyes. "Perhaps if I hadn't protested so strongly..." Tears began to stream down her cheeks.

Ewewyrd tried to console her by patting her tenderly on the shoulder.

"It's not your fault, Freyja. If only Lumpy had listened, none of this would have happened."

Kyle wasn't interested in who was to blame. All he cared about were his two best friends.

"What happened after the giants caught them?"

He swallowed hard, not really sure if he wanted to hear the answer.

Freyja read his mind and said, "Don't worry. They didn't eat them—yet." She forced a nervous smile.

The relief Kyle sensed evaporated in a moment. He narrowed his eyes as he looked accusingly at Ewewyrd.

"How it is that you two managed to escape, but Megan and Lumpy didn't?"

"I don't think they saw us," stammered Ewewyrd. "Or they would have caught us too."

Kyle turned to Freyja for confirmation.

Freyja nodded in agreement.

"We ducked behind some bushes when Megan screamed and stayed there until the giants had finished binding her and Lumpy to the back of a cart. We were so scared we didn't dare move until they were gone."

Kyle saw the fear in her eyes and felt ashamed for thinking ill of his two elf friends.

"It's a good thing the giants didn't see you or they might have captured you too. At least now I know what happened to my friends and we have a better chance to rescue them."

"Huh!" Ewewyrd's jaw dropped.

Kyle wrinkled up his brow in thought.

"But we're going to need the rest of the fairy dust to do so."

"All of it?" squeaked Ewewyrd.

Kyle bobbed his head slowly, deliberately.

"You'll know why once you hear what I have in mind."

Ewewyrd placed a possessive hand on the bag containing the fairy dust as he listened to Kyle outline his plan to rescue Megan and Lumpy.

13
GINNUNGAGAP

FROM THE MOUNTAINS beyond the sea to the farthest reaches of Jotunheim, their greatest stronghold, they came to assemble in a clearing overlooking the once mighty River Thrice and the barren wasteland, Ginnungagap, to join forces and crush the little people. But before the giants could stand united they had to choose a leader, someone to guide them into battle, and there was no shortage of contenders. After days of bitter fighting, where the blood of the losers had turned the waters of the river red, it came down to the last two combatants; Trichrug, the mountain giant, with his double-headed axe, and Brutus, the frost giant, with his spiked club the size of a small tree.

Both combatants stood in the centre of a gory, mud-sodden depression, eyeing each other with undisguised menace, oblivious of the bloodthirsty hoard gathered around them. While Trichrug circled slowly and coolly measured his opponent, Brutus tapped the club, stained red by the blood of his victims, in the palm of his calloused hand. Not as tall as or as broad in the shoulders as the frost giant, Brutus was counting on a cunning mind and superior reflexes to win the day. It wasn't long before his reflexes were put to the test.

With amazing speed Trichrug swung the axe in the air, roaring fiercely as the blade chopped at the club thrown up to block the blow, spraying splinters everywhere. An onlooker whose features were all but hidden behind a black, bushy beard howled in pain when one of the jagged projectiles pierced him in the eye. The crowd roared with delight.

Trichrug lashed out again and again, forcing Brutus to parry and retreat until the latter ran out of room and found himself backed up into the unyielding crowd. The mountain giant noticed some of his own men standing behind his opponent, prodding him with their axes and pushing him forward, and his lips curled up in a grim smile. He moved in for the kill.

The frost giant ducked as the axe swooshed through the air, ruffling his thatch of black hair and neatly removing the head of the fellow standing directly behind him. The severed head hit the ground with a thud and, by the time Trichrug realized he had struck one of his own men, it was too late. Brutus lunged forward unexpectedly and rammed his club in to the pit of Trichrug's stomach. As Trichrug doubled over in pain, the frost giant hammered him on the back of the head.

The crowd uttered an audible groan at the sound of a loud crack and the sight of the mountain giant falling flat on his face in the mud. Blood gushed from a gaping hole in the back of Trichrug's crushed skull, coursing through his matted hair, spilling onto the mucky earth and merging with the red river flowing away from the decapitated body.

For a moment everyone looked on in stunned silence, shocked that the underdog had come out on top. Then, someone in the crowd cheered, and soon more voices rang out in favor of the champion. Before long the whole horde erupted, chanting the name of their new leader. "Brutus. Brutus. Brutus."

Brutus raised the bloody club and said, "By this club I declare myself the victor. If there are any among you who wish to challenge my claim, step forward now." His cruel, dark eyes surveyed the throng.

The crowd fell silent once again. All eyes were glued to the club and some remnants of scalp and brain tissue pasted to one of the spikes. It was a gruesome reminder of what could happen to anyone who accepted the frost giant's challenge. No one stepped forward.

Brutus sniffed disapprovingly.

"Whether you are wise or simply cowards, the truth shall soon be known."

He glanced at the crumpled heap at his feet. "You two," he snarled, jabbing the club at a pair of surly looking characters standing nearby. "Get rid of this, garbage." He spat at the dead mountain giant. "As for the rest of you, there's plenty of work still to be done before we march on Alfheim. I suggest you all get busy."

The crowd dispersed, speaking in murmurs as it broke into smaller groups and headed for the base camps spread out along the riverbank. While some of the camps accommodated as many as a dozen men, most were quite small with no more than two or three in the party. There was a lot of hammering and banging and yelling out orders going on, especially in the larger camps where the great siege weapons had to be readied for battle; catapults, towers, an enormous battering ram. An army of trolls and yak-like beasts slaved away under the watchful eyes of the giants.

It had been several hours since Megan and Lumpy were taken captive and bound to the back of a cart loaded with crossbow bolts as long as a full grown man. Seeing as they arrived at the clearing less than an hour ago, much of the time had been spent scrambling along a rutted trail to keep pace with the mounted giants and to stay one step ahead of the crushing wheels of an enormous crossbow (a.k.a. ballista) being hauled behind them. Lumpy's heart may have stopped pounding shortly after arriving but he was beginning to think his head would remain in a fog forever. He could still hear the ballista rumbling in his ears, making it seem like the ground was still vibrating long after they stopped moving. He endeavored to eavesdrop on a conversation between the hirsute giant left behind to watch over them and one of his comrades returning to the camp to impart news of Brutus' victory, but their deep-throated murmurs were unintelligible due to the persistent drumming in his head.

After listening for awhile and gleaning no information, Lumpy was beginning to get frustrated. He smacked himself on the side of the head to see if he couldn't defog his brain. It seemed to work. He managed to catch some of what they were saying, not that it was of any importance to him, before a third, more officious giant appeared on the scene and interrupted them. The newcomer pointed at Lumpy, while muttering under his breath.

"What about the other one?" the hirsute giant said.

The newcomer regarded Megan with critical eyes.

"That bony thing!" he exclaimed. "Feed her to the trolls."

A cold fear gripped Megan as she realized they were talking about her. She shuddered, recalling the mess the trolls had made when they ripped apart the gnome.

"They're going to feed me to the trolls," she said, crying in Lumpy's ear.

"So I hear" said Lumpy indifferently.

"Isn't there something we can do?"

Lumpy raised his arms to draw attention to the thick rope wrapped around his wrists and fastened to the cart they were seated under. The skin underneath and around the rope was raw, not only from the constant tugging and jerking along the way, but from repeated attempts to escape.

"Not while we have this to contend with."

Megan noticed that the skin around her wrists had faired no better. She buried her head in her hands and wept.

Lumpy seemed to draw strength from Megan's despair, grimacing in pain as he made one last desperate attempt to slip through his bonds. Just when he was ready to admit defeat the rope gave enough to allow him to ease part of his hand through the gap. He cursed his fat thumb for getting in the way.

"Let me help you with that," said a throaty voice in his ear.

Lumpy started at the sound of something so close, and tried to hide his hands from the massive figure standing over him with a dagger. It was the fellow who had been guarding them for the past hour. The giant, who appeared to be alone now, reached down, took him by the hand and sliced through the rope as easy as cutting through butter. He returned the dagger to its scabbard before yanking Lumpy to his feet.

Megan's thoughts were full of foreboding when she saw that Lumpy was about to be taken away. She screamed and wrapped her arms around his legs.

"Take your filthy hands off him!"

The dimwit was so used to taking orders that he actually obeyed. He let go, but only for a moment.

"Hey! Who do you think you are telling me what to do?"

He fixed Lumpy with a crushing grip, tugging on his arm while Megan continued to hold onto his legs.

For all her effort, Megan was dragged along the ground like a dead weight. It wasn't until she reached the end of her rope that the giant actually felt any resistance. The cart groaned as the rope drew taut.

"Let go!" the giant growled. "Or I'll pluck out your innards."

Lumpy was beginning to feel like a New Year's cracker that was ready to explode.

"Someone had better let go and soon," he said behind gritted teeth.

He could hear a lot of snapping and crackling, and thought he was coming apart at the seams. Only when the sounds of a commotion reached his ears and the smell of burning flesh tickled his nose did he understand differently.

The giant was torn between taking Lumpy by force or throwing himself in the mix of giants and lesser beasts scurrying about in the clearing. Not only did the giants have their hands full trying to extinguish a number of blazes that had mysteriously sprung up, the more urgent just now threatening to engulf the enormous crossbow, but they had to keep an eye out for stampeding yaks. Somehow, the beasts had gotten loose and converged on the fodder cart, devouring whatever they could before the whole thing went up in smoke. More than one of the beasts had ventured too close to the blaze and, instead of filling their stomachs they fed the fire, spreading the flames more rapidly throughout the camp. It was a matter of self-preservation when the hirsute giant caught a glimpse of something out of the corner of his eye and turned his head in time to see a roaring fireball barreling towards him.

The giant released Lumpy and leapt aside to avoid being bulled over and possibly set ablaze by a rampaging yak. As he stumbled and fell backward, his head hit the ground with a sickening crack.

Luckily, the hardest thing Lumpy struck when he flew back was Megan's bony body. He heard the wind get knocked out of her as he tumbled over her and rolled under the wagon. When he finally came to rest he sat up, grimacing and rubbing his backside, still tender after his encounter with the sea serpent.

"Are you alright?" Megan asked.

"Of course he is," said a familiar voice. "He landed on his butt."

"Kyle!"

Megan searched everywhere but needless to say she didn't see anything. Then she felt a hand on her wrist, and glanced down to see the giant's dagger floating in midair.

"Don't move!" cautioned Kyle.

Megan held her breath until the dagger cut through the last thread. While she rubbed her wrists to coax the blood to return, she saw the dagger drop on the ground and a powdery substance glitter in the air above her. As the substance rained down on her she felt a slight tingling sensation from her head down to her toes. By the time the feeling had gone away almost half of her body had vanished. She watched in awe as Lumpy was sprinkled and began to disappear as well.

"Grab onto my cloak," whispered Kyle. "And don't let go, no matter what."

Megan felt around blindly and seized his sleeve. Lumpy grabbed hold of Megan just before she vanished completely.

"Good. Now, on the count of three I want you both to stand with me. One. Two. Three."

Their grunts and groans went unnoticed; and so did they. Only the two ropes hanging down from the back of the cart gave their whereabouts away, swaying inexplicably when they brushed past them.

●   ●   ●   ●

The plan worked to perfection, just like Kyle said it would. While Ewewyrd and Freyja started the fires to create a diversion, Kyle calmly released Megan and Lumpy and spirited them away from under the giants' noses. By the time the last flame had been doused and someone had stumbled upon the unconscious guard, Kyle and his two friends had met up with the two elves at a prearranged location and, together, the five of them made for the river.

They would have liked to cross the river at the shallowest point but that would have meant doing so in full view of the giants. And given that the fairy dust would have been washed away as soon as they stepped in the water, they decided to stroll upriver, away from enemy eyes. Eventually they came to a bend in the river and crossed unseen.

On the other side of the river was a narrow stretch of land covered in scrub and, beyond that, sand. Rolling dunes of deep, dry sand for as far as the eye could see.

Kyle gazed long and hard, trying to visualize the mountains he knew were there. But they were either too far away or the dunes simply stood in the way. Feeling a need to wet his throat, he reached down and scooped up a handful of the cool, clear water flowing inexorably downstream. As he drank he couldn't help but notice his blackened hands. He dropped to his knees, staring in horror at the accursed flesh and wailing piteously.

Megan stood watching Kyle, wishing that there was something, anything she could do to lessen the burden. But she realized it was only wishful thinking. The pain and misery brought on by the curse was his load to bear and could not be passed around like some unwanted thing. There was only one way to help, she reasoned, and that was to deal with the self-pity that brought Kyle to his knees; before all hope was lost and he became a victim of his own despair. With that thought in mind she took a determined step towards him.

"Don't you dare give up on us now, Kyle Dunlop! Not after everything we've been through, and all because of you."

It made her feel sick to her stomach to treat him so cruelly, but to her way of thinking, it was the only hope she had of breaking through the wall of gloom he had built up around himself.

Sometimes it takes a good, hard slap in the face to wake a person up and, while Megan may not have actually smacked Kyle, the tongue-lashing she gave him seemed to have the desired effect. Kyle stopped sobbing and lowered his hands so he no longer had to look at them.

"You're right," he said. "It is my fault. But it's not as if I didn't mean well."

Megan placed a reassuring hand on Kyle's shoulder. When next she spoke there was no trace of malice or rebuke in her voice.

"You're intentions have never been in doubt. I knew what they were right from the start. What concerns me now is your desire to see this thing through."

"Megan's right," said Lumpy, as he sloshed through the water and approached Kyle from the other side. "It's not like you to act this way. Maybe the curse is starting to affect your brain."

As much as he hated to admit it, Kyle was thinking the very same thing. The peculiar sensation that sometimes washed over his body like a wave had been increasing in frequency and intensity since that first fateful day. And as the corruption continued to spread right before his eyes, there was no doubt in his mind that much the same was going on inside his body. He was beginning to feel the effects of this in his stomach, where the painful cramps of the last hour or two kept telling him that something wasn't right. He brushed aside his discomfort the same way he brushed aside everything else that had happened to them over the past few days; by focusing on their ultimate objective.

"It won't happen again," he said with renewed spirit and determination. "I promise."

The ghost of a smile appeared on Megan's face. "That's good enough for me."

"Me too," said Lumpy, helping Megan haul Kyle to his feet.

In anticipation of the journey ahead they availed themselves of the river by drinking until they were ready to burst. Satiated to the point of feeling sick, they wound their way around the scrub and took their first tentative steps in the sand. Using the dunes as cover and crouching to keep their heads down, they headed away from the river and the one hundred odd giants assembled on the other side. They thought they were heading away from danger but, in reality, they were merely exchanging one peril for another. Ginnungagap wasn't called 'the yawning void' without good reason.

With no sun above to guide them and surrounded by a sea of sand, they wandered for hours not really knowing which way they were going. They may have been on course for Darkalfheim. Then again, they may have been walking in the wrong direction entirely. One grain of sand was as indistinguishable as another, one dune no different or easier to climb than the others.

Normally, Ewewyrd and Freyja were able to keep pace and match Kyle stride for stride. But the sand was so loose and so deep, and their legs were so skinny, that they sank up to their knees with almost every step they took. By contrast, the sand barely rose above Kyle's ankles. As a result, they were finding it harder and harder to keep up.

"Can't we stop? Just for a few minutes," pleaded Freyja, as Kyle reached the foot of another dune.

She would have been better off saving her breath because even if Kyle had heard what she said it wouldn't have made any difference. He still would have approached the dune with the same energy and dogged determination he had shown from the onset. Sighing wearily, she waited for him to reach the top before reluctantly staggering forward with Ewewyrd at her side.

And so it went. Up and down, one dune after another, with no stops in-between; the same grueling pace, the same droning sound of sand crunching under foot. Perhaps it was good that they didn't stop. With no food or water to satisfy their hunger, quench their thirst, brighten their spirits, it was better to be distracted by the sand than to dwell on every little thing that ailed them.

Eventually, they were forced to halt as nighttime descended and shrouded the dunes in darkness. But just before this happened they stumbled upon some ruins. The dozen or so buildings that peeked out of the sand suggested that the land hereabouts wasn't always so barren and inhospitable. That it had supported life and the life it supported had flourished for a time. They fell asleep, crowded together behind one of the stone walls that used to shelter life, wondering whatever happened to this oasis in the desert.

●   ●   ●   ●

With the arrival of morning came the answer to the question. No sooner had they turned their backs on the ruins than they almost tripped over another group of derelict buildings buried in the sand. A wide depression between the two sites, which ran parallel to one another, marked the location of a dried up riverbed. The life sustaining water had long since receded, forcing the inhabitants to abandon their homes and making way for the sand to move in and claim the land.

Kyle considered this discovery with mixed emotions. On the one hand he was glad for a sign that indicated they were on the right track, since there was no doubt in his mind that the river on Brokk's map and the dried up river were one and the same. On the other hand, he was disappointed and troubled by what he saw. Without water, the river he had set out to reach was absolutely useless. Not only would it be impossible to proceed at the same torrid pace as yesterday, but it was going to become increasing difficult to continue once their muscles started to cramp up from dehydration. He kept these thoughts to himself as he guided the others past the ruins and ambled up to the first dune of the day.

Needless to say they labored from the onset, unable to shake off the aches and pains that had settled in overnight. Each dune they stumbled upon seemed to get bigger and bigger, the sand beneath their feet deeper and deeper, their legs heavier and heavier. And as they breathed in the dusty, arid air their throats became parched, as dry as the sand itself.

Kyle trudged up the side of an agonizingly long dune, pausing at the top to catch his breath and comb the horizon. Through prickling eyes he saw something in the distance that warranted a closer look, only a sharp cry kept him from focusing in right away. He glanced over his shoulder to see Freyja lying in a heap at the foot of the dune. He watched Ewewyrd bend down, take Freyja in his insubstantial arms, and strive to lift her.

For a moment it looked like the elf was going to carry her up the hill himself, but even before he took the first tentative step signs of strain began to show on his face. His knees started to wobble and his legs quickly buckled under the extra weight. He fell backward. With Freyja sprawled out across his chest, all that could be seen of him were his legs and arms poking out of the sand.

Mercifully, Lumpy tramped down the hill and hoisted Freyja off him. As Lumpy slung Freyja over his shoulder and turned to tackle the hill, Ewewyrd dug himself out of the sand. He brushed at the granules still stuck to his tattered sackcloth tunic. Then he humped up the hill after Lumpy.

Rubbing the grit from his eyes, Kyle gazed across the gleaming sand until the distant images, blurred by sweat and grime, began to take shape; mountains. He threw up his arms and uttered a jubilant cry. "Yes."

His exuberance spilled over as he spotted Megan advancing towards him. Pouncing on her, he wrapped his arms around her meager waist, lifted her off her feet and swung her round a full three hundred and sixty degrees before collapsing, exhausted, in the sand.

Lumpy didn't know what to think when he crested the dune and saw them both lying side by side in the sand. At first he thought they had keeled over due to exhaustion. Then he noticed the exultant look on Kyle's face.

"It's nice to see that at least some of us are enjoying the experience," he said, placing Freyja down on a soft bed of sand then collapsing at their feet.

Kyle sat upright and pointed, directing Lumpy's attention to a distant land beyond the sandy sea.

"Look! We're almost there".

Lumpy squinted but the mountains were so far away the only thing he could discern was the outline of several peaks.

"We haven't made it yet," he said wearily. "And some of us might not make it at all." He regarded Freyja gravely.

Freyja was unconscious, her chest rising and falling ever so slightly as her life dangled by a thread. There was a pasty look to her skin that wasn't the least bit healthy and her lips were slightly blue.

Kyle gave a wan smile and climbed to his feet.

"Don't worry. We'll make it even if I have to carry each and every one of you the rest of the way myself."

He walked over to where Freyja lay comatose on the sand and tried to lift her up onto his shoulder. Lumpy saw his friend struggling and, although he had just made himself comfortable, he reluctantly got to his feet and bumped Kyle aside lightly.

"Leave her to me," said Lumpy. "You can carry the next one who drops— which just might be me."

Kyle gladly concurred, leaving Lumpy to scoop up Freyja in his beefy arms. While he plodded down the hill, Lumpy, Megan and Ewewyrd stepped in line behind him.

Two hours later they were still no closer to their objective. At least that's the impression they got as the sand and the dunes gradually gave way to a rock-hard plain that seemed to go on forever. Deep cracks scarred the landscape, making the flat, barren surface look like a giant jigsaw puzzle. The hazy mountains teased them from afar; elusive and aloof.

One by one they dropped. First it was Megan. Then Lumpy, with Ewewyrd and Freyja tucked loosely under his arms. Finally, after dragging his feet for another minute or so, Kyle's legs gave way underneath him and he fell. He found the strength to roll over onto his back but wasn't able to budge after that. Defeated, he turned his head to gaze upon the distant mountains one last time and, through glazed eyes, he saw a cloud of dust rising up from the plain.

14
ALFHEIM

"WELL?"

"He's alive but just barely," said a tall, sinewy elf with shoulder length blonde hair, intelligent blue eyes, and pointed ears, much like Ewewyrd and Freyja. His striking features were enhanced by a golden necklet and two gold bands, one wrapped around each wrist, and a padded navy blue tunic gathered at his tapered waist with a leather belt. The belt's golden buckle sparkled so brilliantly it seemed to emit a light of its own.

"What about the others?"

"The same, my lord," a second elf replied.

As the speaker stood after examining Freyja, his long shadow fell over the unconscious maiden like a death robe. He repositioned the longbow slung over his left shoulder so that it sat more comfortably across his broad back and waited patiently for further instructions.

Had the second elf not called his questioner "lord", there would have been no way of knowing that Fairrain was the leader. He and his band of warrior elves were identical in every respect, down to the clothes they wore, the weapons they carried and the majesty of their pure white steeds.

"Give him a sip of this," said Fairrain, reaching into a saddle bag and pulling out a wrinkled wineskin. "Then see to the others." He tossed the container to the first elf he had spoken to.

The elf snatched the wineskin out of midair. Then he unplugged the container, knelt down beside Kyle, raised his head off the hard ground and poured a few drops of the translucent liquid on his chapped lips.

Kyle ran a dry tongue over his wetted lips, making a face at the fiery taste. He made to turn his head away.

Strengthening his grip, the elf forced Kyle's head round and held it steady while he crammed the wineskin in his reluctant mouth. He squeezed the container tightly.

Kyle coughed and sputtered, expelling the liquid, but not before some of it managed to slide down his parched throat and achieve the desired result. As he slowly regained consciousness, the warrior elf went around to the others and repeated the process.

By the time the elf was done administering the tonic, everyone, with the exception of Freyja, had recovered enough to ride double behind one of the warriors. Since she was still too weak to hold on, Freyja had to sit up front between a sturdy pair of arms.

To make up for lost time, Fairrain sped off at a gallop, setting the pace for the others to follow. Soon, Kyle and his companions were on the move again.

As the horses dashed across the open plain Kyle noticed that the foothills he and his companions had failed to reach were on the left and, while they didn't seem any farther away, they certainly weren't getting any closer. He pictured the map he had ingrained in his head and quickly realized they were going in the wrong direction. Horror-struck, he croaked in the elf's ear. "You're going the wrong..." His voice faltered and he had to swallow to moisten his dry throat. "We need to go that way." He tapped the fellow on the shoulder and pointed to the mountains on his left. "That way..." He felt a tickle in his throat and almost coughed himself out of the saddle. When he finally finished coughing his throat was too sore and his voice was too hoarse to say another word. Not that it would have mattered. The warrior elf had one thing on his mind and that was to keep up with the lead rider.

•   •   •   •

They rode hard for what seemed like an eternity, eventually putting the mountains behind them and heading for an unknown destination in the upper right-hand corner of Brokk's map. The landscape couldn't have been more bleak, and their prospects more grim.

Saddle bruised and weary, Kyle was beginning to wish Fairrain had left him behind to die in peace. Anything, he thought, would have been better than bouncing about on the hard, unpadded seat. He groaned as the horse cleared a deep crevice in the dry, pitted earth, landing heavily and rattling every bone in his body. He was wondering how much more punishment he would have to endure when the elf finally tightened the reins. Peering over the warrior's shoulder, he was able to see for himself why they had suddenly stopped.

Sprouting from the ground like a humungous wart was a flat plateau, topped to a large extent by an imposing, double-walled fortress. The back and sides of the outer wall abutted the sheer cliff face, with turrets in each corner overlooking the plain below. The remaining side was divided in two by a raised drawbridge, and fronted by a wide ditch filled with scummy water. Beyond the ditch was a narrow stretch of bare rock sloping downward to a long flight of broad steps carved into the plateau from top to bottom.

As Fairrain guided the riders up the stone steps, the drawbridge creaked and groaned open. Descending slowly, the massive structure thudded to the ground on the other side of the ditch.

The horses charged across the drawbridge to the cheers of all those waiting within.

Fairrain sought a face in the crowd and, when he found who he was searching for, he smiled and dismounted. However before he was able to approach the individual a wide-eyed boy smelling strongly of horses rushed to his side, eager to tend to his mount.

The warrior elf stroked the horse's muzzle and patted the sweaty beast gently before handing over the reins.

"Don't be afraid to spoil her, lad."

"I will at that, my lord."

The boy led the exhausted horse away to be stabled.

The interruption allowed the individual Fairrain had acknowledged to move forward until he was standing directly in front of the warrior elf. The stranger extended his hand in greeting.

"Welcome to Alfheim, brother."

The stranger's otherwise handsome face was haggard and strained, and there was a look of despair in his weary, blood-shot eyes.

Fairrain clasped the hand tightly and pulled his older brother and heredity ruler of Alfheim towards him. He wrapped one brawny arm then the other around his sibling's back and held him closely. A tear ran down his check.

"It's been a long time, Eridaal," he whispered in his brother's ear. "I only wish we were meeting under different circumstances."

Eridaal returned his brother's warm embrace. Through misty eyes he said, "It's comforting to know you and your men will be by our side."

They parted but not before Fairrain gave the king a respectful kiss on both cheeks.

The king regarded Fairrain's men, raising an inquisitive eye at the five oddballs in the group. He bobbed his head in greeting at Kyle before saying to everyone, "Lord Fairrain and I have a lot to discuss. In the meantime, you are all welcome to eat at my table."

While the two leaders went off to discuss strategy, the crowd delighted in escorting Fairrain's retinue to the great hall, where everyone who attended was treated to the best the kitchen had to offer. After stuffing themselves to the gills, Kyle and his companions retired for the evening, leaving the others to revel well into the early hours of the morning.

Since space was at a premium in Alfheim, they found themselves occupying a room above the noisy great hall. In spite of the loud voices and raucous laughter emanating through the floorboards they were too tired to hear a thing and, within minutes of bedding down on the hard floor, for there were no beds in the room, they were all fast asleep.

Morning came sooner than expected when Kyle was jolted awake by a severe headache and sharp abdominal pains. He folded like a cheap seat, clutching his stomach and stifling a moan. With the others still slumbering, he waited for the pain to subside before sinking his teeth into the sleeve of his cloak and bolting out of the room.

Dashing along the corridor, he fled down a flight of stairs and burst through a side exit; and not a moment too soon. He didn't know what was more agonizing, the gut wrenching cramps that threatened to bring him to his knees or the sight of all that wonderful food from the night before splattering at his feet.

Once he was through retching he made his way to the communal well. Situated in a courtyard just inside the gated entrance of the inner wall, the well, which must have been painstakingly excavated, was equidistant from the three buildings that dominated the inner quarter. The royal palace, by far the most imposing, stood front and centre. It was flanked by barracks on one side and the officers' quarters on the other side. Many of the lesser buildings obscured from view served as workshops and smithies, storehouses, and living quarters for the general populace.

Kyle turned a crank, lowering the bucket fastened to a thick rope. Only after most of the rope was uncoiled did he hear a faint splash. He waited for the bucket to fill up with water before reeling it in. Once the bucket was within reach he grabbed it and poured the cold water over his grungy hair, taking in a mouthful, gargling and spitting to wash away the bad taste in his mouth. He was about to replace the bucket when he was startled by the sound of clacking heels.

He froze, hoping that if he didn't move or make a sound no one would even notice he was there. It must have worked, because Lord Fairrain and King Eridaal, along with two armed attendants, strode by without so much as glancing in his direction. He overheard the king say, "At least they're willing to parley." Curious, he waited for the gates to swing open and the king and his party to exit before chasing after them.

To his surprise, there was already a flurry of activity beyond the inner wall. While one group of warrior elves rolled a massive catapult into the clearing the crowd had gathered in the other day, a much larger group used a block and tackle to hoist a ballista, slightly smaller than the massive crossbow he saw in the giant camp, onto one of the turrets. Out of the clamor came the sound of winches creaking and metal chains rattling as the drawbridge was lowered for the king.

Kyle thought about following the king's party further but he was afraid that someone might stop him and question his intentions. Instead, he moved furtively along the inner wall until he was standing opposite a staircase built into the outer wall. He crossed the clearing and climbed the steep steps, hoping that no one had observed him. Even if someone had, he thought, they were too busy to pay much attention to him.

At the top of the staircase was a parapet that overlooked the plain below. Peeking through a crenellation he was stunned by what he saw.

While Alfheim slept the giants crept into position, creating a blockade by completely surrounding the plateau. Like a plague of locusts in a wheat field the plain was beset by giants, trolls and other beasts of burden, war machines, weapons carts, and anything else the giants needed to besiege the fortress. Sure, everything was quiet now, but Kyle knew the calm wouldn't last. Once the giants had time to recover from the long, grueling trek they would awaken refreshed, lusting for blood. A cold fear gripped him.

Near the base of the plateau, just beyond the broad stone steps leading up to Alfheim, a tent had been erected. A giant standing guard scowled fiercely and gave a guttural growl as the king and his party approached.

Fairrain reached for his sword but Eridaal put a hand on the hilt before the weapon made it too far out of the scabbard. Grudgingly, Fairrain let the sword slide back in the scabbard and removed his clenched fist.

Reluctantly, the giant, who stood twice as high as Fairrain, stepped aside to allow the king and his party to enter the tent. Fairrain curled his lip in disgust as he strode past the guard.

With one eye on the tent and the other eye on the turret, Kyle wondered if his luck was once again going to take a turn for the worse. In his mind's eye he saw the giant army storming the fortress, smashing through the drawbridge and the gates of the inner wall, and ripping apart every man, women and child. Then boiling the flesh in huge cauldrons and smacking their lips contently as they gorged themselves on elf and human stew. He was roused from his reverie by an agonizing scream.

The cries of pain that followed were so intense that even the men on the turret paused to gape. But only those with a clear view of the tent were able to see and surmise for themselves what might have happened, as Eridaal and Fairrain rushed out of the pavilion unaccompanied. They made an undignified dash for the plateau, thunderous laughter chasing them up the broad steps to the drawbridge. Needless to say, this did nothing to dispel Kyle's fears.

As the drawbridge rattled upward, Eridaal summoned the officer overseeing the installation of the ballista. The officer promptly left someone else in charge, then hastened to the king's side. His creased face turned grave whilst he listened to what the king had to say. Before departing, Eridaal placed a comforting hand on his shoulder and the two men spent a moment to grieve together in silence.

It took a minute for the officer to regain his composure, but once he had absorbed the shock of losing his only son he vented his new found fury on everyone in sight.

"Is that any way to prepare for battle? By standing around gawking? Get back to work, now!"

The soldiers, who were still catching their breath after struggling with the catapult, almost tripped over each other as they scrambled to find something else to do. Meanwhile, the officer went back to what he was doing earlier; shouting out orders to the men on the turret.

"Put your backs into it you slackers. Can't you see we've got a war to fight?"

News of the blockade and the one day window the king was given to contemplate surrendering unconditionally spread like wildfire. Soon, every soul within the fortress walls was up and about doing his or her part to help Alfheim gear up for war. Megan and Freyja tore up sheets to make bandages for the inevitable casualties. Then they lent a hand in the kitchen. Kyle and Lumpy transferred armloads of barbed arrows from a storage shed to the battlements running along both walls. Ewewyrd hauled around a bucket offering water and a brief reprieve to the tireless workers.

At one point Ewewyrd's oversized ears overheard someone mention the word "secret tunnel". While several of the king's men unloading a cartload of boulders to be used as missiles stopped to quench their thirst, he eavesdropped on a conversation between two youths. Lacking the strength to handle the huge boulders themselves, the boys contributed to the cause by tending to the needs of the two drooling beasts of burden hitched up to the cart.

"How come I never heard about any secret tunnel?" said the bigger boy, as he held up a bucket and tipped it towards one of the beasts. A big red tongue lapped up the water inside.

The smaller boy shrugged his narrow shoulders.

"Don't ask me. Maybe you're not supposed to know."

Even though his bucket was only half full, the smaller boy found that it was too heavy to hold up. Rather than bother to try, he set it on the ground and made the other beast bend down to drink.

The bigger boy glared at the smaller boy.

"Hey. What's that supposed to mean?"

Unwittingly, the bigger boy tilted the bucket too much and water sloshed at his feet. He righted the bucket but not before the beast showed its displeasure by butting him with a wet nose.

"Nothing," the smaller boy said. "It's just that my dad is an important officer. And your dad is..."

His voice trailed off, but the bigger boy understood perfectly well what he meant. It wasn't the first time the smaller boy knew more than he did just because his father happened to be a high ranking official, not a lowly archer.

As much as the bigger boy would have liked to sock the smaller boy in the nose, his curiosity got the better of him and he found himself asking, "Alright, mister know-it-all. Where is it?"

The smaller boy hesitated, wondering if it was wise to reveal the secret. He relented when he noticed the look of doubt on the other boy's face.

"In the well," he said, regarding his friend with smug satisfaction.

The bigger boy thought about this for a moment but he didn't see how it could be possible. He must have peered down the well a hundred times, dropping a pebble and making a wish, but never once did he come across any sign of a secret tunnel.

"Is this another one of your lies?" he said, frowning severely.

Bothered by the suggestion, the smaller boy slapped both arms across his chest and said, "May Odin strike me dead if it is."

They both looked skyward but nothing happened.

"Hey you!"

Ewewyrd started backwards at the sound of a voice in his ear and turned to find a mallet sized fist in his face. His eyes widened in fear. Then he noticed the wooden cup clasped in the clenched fist and he let out a sigh of relief.

"We're done," said a brawny figure, looming large and peering down at Ewewyrd. He dropped the empty cup in the bucket. It hit the bottom with a thud.

Ewewyrd smiled wanly, waiting for the warrior elf to rejoin the others before rushing off to tell Kyle the good news. A few minutes later he spotted both Kyle and Lumpy on the battlement circling the inner wall. He saw them drop off an armload of arrows, then head for a flight of steps, in a hurry to get more. It was hard to contain his excitement as he watched them descend.

"You're just the fellow I wanted to see," said Lumpy, snatching the cup and scooping out air. "Hey! It's empty." He tossed the cup back inside the bucket, glaring at Ewewyrd in the process.

Kyle could tell by the nervous twitch in his eyes that Ewewyrd had something to say.

"Quiet! I think Ewewyrd wants to tell us something."

Lumpy huffed and crossed his arms.

Ignoring Lumpy, Ewewyrd told Kyle about the conversation he overheard and the secret tunnel. Since there was no way of proving or disproving the boy's claim without actually climbing inside the well, Kyle decided to wait until nighttime to investigate. Only then, under the cover of darkness, would they be able to see for themselves what was down there. Assuming the boy wasn't fibbing, they would have plenty of time to slip away before morning.

For the next little while Kyle's mind was on something other than the task he had been assigned and, although he worked like a fiend, placing arrows at strategic points along the battlement and then pouring bucket loads of black tarry goop into holding tubs, he planned their escape down to the last detail. Among other things, he made a mental list of the things they would need, not only to escape from Alfheim, but to survive the journey across the plain: a torch, some food and water, a rope and perhaps a knife or two for protection. And when they finally managed to meet in private later in the day he thought it was going to be a simple matter of sharing his plan with the others and making arrangements to procure the items on the list. He couldn't have been more wrong.

"What do you mean you're not coming?"

They were sitting in a circle in a dusty corner of the kitchen, as far as possible from the heat of the oven that Megan and Freyja had slaved over for the better part of the morning. They were supposed to be enjoying the midday meal. Everyone else was. At least, that was the intention. A handful of frosty stares pointed in their direction suggested otherwise. Kyle tugged on Ewewyrd's arm, making the elf sit down after he had jumped to his feet and screeched across the circle at Freyja.

"I'm tired of running," said Freyja. "I want to stay here where it's safe."

"Safe!" cried Ewewyrd. "How can you possibly feel safe here?"

He was so agitated he started to break out in a cold sweat. Tiny beads left a slick trail down either side of his face.

Freyja reached out and squeezed Ewewyrd's hand hard enough to make him wince.

"Keep your voice down," she said softly. "Do you want everyone to hear us?"

Ewewyrd looked around, surprised to see how many heads were turned their way. He lowered his impassioned voice.

"By this time tomorrow this place is going to be crawling with giants. If you stay here, you'll die."

"Maybe it will. Maybe it won't," said Freyja. "That's a chance I'm willing to take." She squeezed his hand more gently, gazing beseechingly into his eyes. "And if you care for me as much as you say you do, you'll stay behind with me."

As much as Ewewyrd adored Freyja, he had a plan of his own; a plan that would bring him that much closer to fulfilling a dream. Afraid of losing her, but even more afraid of losing sight of his dream, he found himself at a loss for words. His lips quivered but nothing came out. He turned to Kyle for support.

Kyle put a hand on Ewewyrd's shoulder.

"Freyja's right. You're better off here, where you have plenty to eat, a warm bed to curl up in, and strong walls to protect you. That's all gone the moment you step outside the city." He glanced at his disfigured hands, hoping to draw attention to them. "If I had the choice, I'd be staying too. But, as you can see, I don't. "

"So would I," said Lumpy. "This is the best stew I've ever tasted." He slopped up the dregs with a slab of bread, which he promptly popped into his cavernous mouth. Then he licked his fingers clean and smacked his lips most agreeably. "In fact, I think I'll grab seconds before it all disappears."

His muscles had tightened up while he was sitting on the hard stone floor so he didn't get to his feet as swiftly as usual. And when he did finally rise, he stretched his aching back before making his way to the pot simmering on the other side of the room. The delay was enough to save his life. One moment the pot was hanging from a chain over the fire. A moment later it was flying through the air, heading straight for him. He hit the floor just as the pot and shards of stone and mortar whizzed by his ears.

Sounds of mass hysteria and painful moans filled the air. Through it all Lumpy heard his name.

He raised his head and peered through the dust at a gaping hole in the wall. A huge boulder was smoldering in the fire the stew had been simmering over. Bodies were strewn everywhere. Some partially buried beneath the rubble. Others seriously burned. Some gravely injured.

Others suffered only minor cuts and bruises. Those fortunate enough to escape unscathed were scrambling to help the injured. One of them was Freyja. After making sure that Lumpy was alright, she rushed to the aid of a youngster bleeding from a deep gash over his eye.

Kyle reached down and helped Lumpy to his feet.

"So much for the truce," said Lumpy, brushing at his dusty clothes.

"They must have finally clued in," said Kyle. "Even an idiot could see the king was gearing up for war, not getting ready to surrender."

A loud boom shook the walls, jarring loose more of the stonework and playing on frazzled nerves. Megan screamed in Kyle's ear.

Kyle stuck a finger in his ear and wiggled it around.

"I don't like the sound of that," he said uneasily. "If one of those missiles hits the well and blocks that tunnel we'll be stuck here forever."

"I doubt the giants will let us live that long," said Ewewyrd gloomily.

"I'm too young to die," cried Megan.

Lumpy ripped a torch off the wall.

"Then I suggest we stop yapping and make a run for it now. With all the chaos and confusion, no one will even notice we're missing."

Without waiting to see what the others would do, Lumpy headed for the exit. Kyle and Megan followed right away. Ewewyrd hesitated, gazing pleadingly at Freyja.

"Are you sure you won't come with us?" His eyes clouded over because he already knew what Freyja was going to say.

Tears streamed down Freyja's face. She had to struggle to speak. "I can't." She lowered her head, so she didn't have to see the hurt in his eyes. The next time she looked up Ewewyrd was gone.

The scene outside was one of bedlam as the panic-stricken citizens ran around in complete disarray, scrambling to avoid the fiery boulders swooshing through the air and slamming with explosive power into anything that got in the way. Voices rang out seeking to bring about some sense of order but much of what was said got lost in the din.

Ewewyrd emerged from the palace just as a flaming missile whizzed through the air and hit the ground in front of him with a thud. He jumped backwards inside the building, ducking behind the wall moments before the missile shot through the main entrance, rumbled across the tiled foyer and crashed through a far wall, leaving behind a path of destruction in its wake.

Upon re-emerging, he saw Megan and Lumpy standing near the well. Lumpy was holding the winch handle securely and slowly letting out the rope. Megan was peering over the side. There was no doubt in his mind where Kyle had disappeared to. As he approached the well he heard a hollow voice say excitedly, "I found it!" A moment later the rope went slack and Lumpy started to frantically turn the crank the other way.

"Your turn," said Lumpy to Megan, when the empty bucket appeared, clunking against the side of the well.

Megan regarded the bucket with trepidation. She leaned forward and reached for the rope, but recoiled after viewing the dizzying black hole beneath her.

Lumpy swung the bucket towards her.

"Either you get in there now, or I chuck you over the side." He flashed a roguish smile at the thought of tossing her in the well.

A section of the inner wall exploded, showering the courtyard with rocks. Screaming in terror, Megan leapt onto the well wall and into the bucket all in one motion. With little more than her feet in the bucket, she wrapped her arms around the rope and squeezed her eyes shut as she descended.

Once Lumpy had lowered Megan and Ewewyrd into the well he grasped the rope, pulled himself up onto the wall, and carefully stepped off until he was suspended in midair. The winch creaked and the support beam began to bend, and for a moment it looked like the whole thing was going to come apart at the seams but, as much as it grumbled and groaned, it managed to remain intact. Sighing heavily, he began the long descent.

•   •   •   •

While the catapults continued to pound the inner bailey, a team of trolls wearing metal breastplates and simple leather helmets dragged a long, wooden platform up the stone steps. They were followed closely by two giants in full body armor, brandishing whips that cracked fiercely and licked at the beasts' bare backs. The trolls roared and squealed in pain as the whips slashed at them from behind, and arrows rained down relentlessly from the front and sides, piercing unprotected flesh.

Bloodied and exhausted, the trolls crested the plateau and were closing in on the ditch when one of the beasts was dropped by a huge crossbow bolt. The barbed head ripped through the breastplate like it was made of tin foil, poking out of the troll's back.

The elves on the battlement cheered. Then they readied the ballista for the next shot. But before they had time to draw back the bow cord an enormous boulder smashed into the turret, taking out part of the wall, the ballista and everyone in its path.

Back on the plateau, a double-headed axe slashed through the air, hacking at a rope fastened to a neck restraint, and a giant foot booted the dead troll aside so the rest of the team could proceed unimpeded.

Even as the elves continued to pelt the trolls with arrows, they managed to reach the ditch. Bleeding profusely, the trolls leapt in the murky water and hauled the platform across the gap, forming a bridge by resting the far end on a rocky lip. Mission accomplished, one of the giants raised a horn to his mouth.

The horn blast was followed by an eerie rumbling sound that emanated from a battering ram so massive it had to be towed by six giants in heavy armor. Twice that number pushed from the sides or behind. The siege weapon thumped up the steps, rolled onto the plateau and thundered across open ground to the makeshift bridge.

Standing on the inner battlement, Eridaal watched in horror as the battering ram crashed into the drawbridge, splitting the wood and making the outer wall shake. As the giants rolled the machine back and prepared to strike again, he gave the order to retreat.

So while the giants kept up the assault on the drawbridge the elves put down their bows and arrows, which were useless against the heavy armor, and came down from the outer wall in droves. They fled through narrow portals discreetly hidden in the inner wall. Once everyone had made it safely to the other side, the stones that had been temporarily removed were put back in place so that there was no sign of the openings.

Barricaded behind the inner wall, the elves waited and watched as the drawbridge trembled with every blow. To a man, they clung to the hope that it would hold out forever no matter what the giants threw at it. But their hopes were quickly dashed when the wood splintered. A moment later the drawbridge exploded and the pointed end of the battering ram peeked through a small opening. Numbed by fear, the elves prepared themselves for the deluge that would follow once the hole was enlarged.

It took several more blows to rent a hole in the drawbridge large enough for the first giant to squeeze through. Before long the outer quarter was crawling with the fiends. A few ran around waving clubs, ready to pulverize any stray elves they could find. The rest chopped at the wooden gates with double-headed axes.

The outcome seemed inevitable until a pair of unrelated events turned the tide in favor of the elves. The first came with a splash when the order was given to tip the holding vats containing the black tarry goop. Spilling through the openings of the crenelated battlement and splattering to the ground, the goop not only spread out in thick waves, but it adhered to anything it came in contact with, including hair, unprotected skin and clothes. By the time the giants realized what was up it was too late; fiery arrows rained down on them, igniting the highly combustible goop and engulfing them in flames.

At the same time the giants trapped in the inferno were writhing in agony, a deafening roar announced the arrival of the second event; dragons. Six enormous shadows sped across the courtyard as the vicious-looking serpents soared over the fortress. Mounted on each beast was a dragon master from the realm of Darkalfheim. Since time immemorial the dark elves have reared and trained the dragons to protect their underground mines, forges and metalworks from treasure hunters and thieves.

Fairrain thought he had wasted valuable time when he made a detour through the mountains of Darkalfheim to ask the dwarves for assistance, but as he watched the fearsome dragons fall from the sky he knew his gamble was about to pay off. The dragons, although there were only a handful of them, were a formidable force. One the giants weren't prepared to face.

Cries of agony rang out as the dragons strafed the plain with jets of fire. One pass after another until the air was ripe with the stench of burning flesh. Before long, the serpents had decimated the invading army and, any giant lucky enough to escape the carnage kept running, without so much as glancing back. In the end, two dragons and their masters lay among the smoldering corpses.

The four remaining dragons circled once to the cheers of the grateful elves strung out along the inner wall or gathered in the courtyard below. Then, just as suddenly as they appeared, they disappeared, behind a pall of black smoke rising up from the battlefield.

15
MUSPELHEIM

THE SECRET PASSAGE was stuffy and cramped, so Kyle and the others had to crawl along on all fours. Despite the discomfort, however, no one complained. They would rather suffer a few scrapes and bruises than suffer at the hand of the giants. As they travelled downward, agonizingly slow, it seemed as if the tunnel would go on forever. They never, for a moment, expected it to end abruptly.

Stifling a groan, Kyle waved the torch he had taken with him at a large boulder blocking the way, lacing the tunnel with dancing shadows. A draught caressed his cheek and a shaft of orange light gave the promise that the end was near. Eager to put the airless passage behind him, he put the torch down and pushed with all his might.

At first the obstacle refused to budge. Then it gave a bit, grating noisily and admitting a rush of fresh air. With a little persistence he managed to roll the boulder clear of the opening. It came to rest against a gnarled bush.

The first thing he noticed when he poked his head out was that the entrance lay hidden behind a wall of dense scrub. With Megan scratching at his legs, itching to clamber over him, he exited, scurrying along the ground to the edge of the living wall. Before long, the others had emerged and were crouched alongside him.

"What's that horrible smell?" said Megan, screwing her nose up and turning to Lumpy with a disgusted look on her face.

"Why do you always have to look at me?" said Lumpy.

"Death," Ewewyrd announced in an unsettling voice.

Megan glimpsed the terror in the elf's eyes and a shiver ran up her spine.

Kyle put a finger to his lips and hissed at them to be quiet.

"Listen."

They turned their heads, ears straining for the faintest sound, but nothing came their way. The plain was as silent and as unsettling as the grave.

"That's strange," said Megan. "I can't hear a thing."

"Me neither," said Ewewyrd.

He wiggled a finger in one of his bat-like ears, dug out a glob of wax and listened afresh, but still there was nothing. Perplexed, he squeezed through a gap in the bushes and quickly vanished from sight.

Kyle, Megan and Lumpy heard the bushes rustle as Ewewyrd slowly made his way to the other side. After a moment of silence the bushes rustled more vigorously. All of a sudden he reappeared, close to where he had entered. His sunken chest was heaving in and out.

"I told you," he said, with eyes so round it looked like they might pop out of their sockets. "Death is all around us."

Megan gasped. Fear made her heart pound like a drum.

"It's not what you think," Ewewyrd said to reassure her. "Come and see for yourself."

He slipped through the bushes once again, only this time the others followed close behind him.

Disbelieving eyes looked up and down the silent plain, sickened by the grisly sight. Despite the loathsome nature of the giants it was hard not to feel a certain amount of pity for the blackened, twisted corpses that littered the smoke-filled battlefield. Kyle caught a whiff of the pungent odor that permeated the air and gagged.

Burying his face in the cloak, he wandered among the faceless corpses. Every now and again he stumbled upon a troll or a yak-like beast, burnt to a crisp, or a siege machine still burning fiercely. It was obvious by the extent of death and destruction around him that an awesome force had been at work here; a single minded force with one goal in mind — total annihilation. As he came around to the front of the fortress he saw that that goal had been realized. He also saw the battered remains of one of the creatures responsible.

A few days ago he would have been stunned by what he saw. But nothing surprised him anymore—goblins, elves, trolls, giants—they are all part of the norm here. And, so it would appear, are dragons. He gazed at the fearsome teeth framing the reptilian mouth and wondered where the enormous, vicious-looking monster had come from. An upward glance revealed nothing, only a pall of black smoke hanging in the still air over Alfheim.

"What do you think happened?" said Megan, coughing as she choked on the smoke rising up from some charred remains.

"It would appear," said Kyle thoughtfully, "that this creature and many more just like came to the aid of Eridaal and his people. Why they would want to do that is beyond me."

He turned to Ewewyrd for a possible explanation but the elf merely shrugged his shoulders, glancing back at him with a blank expression.

"There's another one over there," said Lumpy pointing towards the plateau. They followed the path of his outstretched hand to a twisted heap near the base of the steps. Scythe-like claws extended skyward, looking almost as menacing now as when the bat-winged monster soared through the air terrorizing the giants. If not for the deep gash in its chest and the giant crossbow bolt peeking out, they might have thought it was asleep. As tempting as it may have been, no one bothered to rush over and rub its leathery stomach.

They proceeded in silence, putting Alfheim behind them and threading their way due west, as Kyle saw it, through the smoldering remnants of the giant army. With any luck there would be no further delays and they would reach the mountain range some time tomorrow to begin the last leg of their journey. Assuming the mountains were passable, there should be more than enough time to locate the river on Brokk's map and follow it straight into the heart of Darkalfheim.

●　　　●　　　●　　　●

After spending a restless night crouched behind a rocky outcrop, they awakened early and set out as soon as there was enough light to see clearly. Anticipation quickly turned to despair as the hours slipped away and they seemed no closer to their objective than when they started.

Hopelessly weary, Kyle began to have doubts about the direction they were headed. What if they had unwittingly strayed off course and, instead of moving towards the mountains they were rambling closer and closer to the barren wasteland. To his dismay, he thought he saw the dunes rising up in the distance. Luckily, Megan and Lumpy saw things differently and promptly laid his doubts to rest.

"I think I see the mountains," said Megan with enthusiasm.

"That's them alright," said Lumpy in a more subdued manner. "But don't get too excited. We've still got a lot of walking to do before we get there."

The sight of the mountains seemed to lift their spirits and give them something to look forward to. Something less tiresome and dreary than the dried up, broken landscape they had been staring at for hours. Eyes to the ground, they picked up the pace.

By late afternoon the mountains began to loom large, and there was a noticeable change in the feel and shape of the land. A sprinkling of sand filled in the cracks nicely, making the ground smoother and easier to walk on. Gently rolling hills broke the monotony without unduly stressing tired, aching muscles.

As they wandered deeper and deeper into the foothills, bubbling pools of fetid scummy water provided a springboard for life, but provided no relief for dusty, parched throats. They would have to trudge on for several more hours before relief finally came their way in the form of a tepid spring with a slight mineral tinge.

The spring was an oasis for a variety of fungi and a lustrous yellow and black speckled slug with a passion for one particularly colorful mushroom. As the gluttonous bugs feasted on the succulent plants their bloated bodies expanded like balloons filling up with air. Slugs at various stages of gluttony were scattered everywhere. Some of them were so grossly misshapen it was a wonder they hadn't burst.

Lumpy wetted his lips, staring longingly at the mushrooms. So far all he and the others had been able to do was slake their thirst. But when his riotous stomach refused to stop grumbling he knew he had to offer it something more substantial. Foreseeing no real danger, he reached down to pick one of the tantalizing delicacies.

Ewewyrd let out a strangled scream and hurled himself bodily at Lumpy. Needless to say, he bounced off the burly teen, hitting the ground with a thump.

"Hey, what's the big idea?" said Lumpy.

He threw the flattened elf a disapproving look.

Winded, Ewewyrd gulped at the air like a fish out of water. "Don't... touch...them," he gasped between gulps. "They're...deadly."

Lumpy gazed longingly at the mushroom he had his heart set on.

"Are you sure? You're not just saying that because you want them all for yourself?"

"Positive," groaned Ewewyrd, rubbing his bruised shoulder. "Try one of those over there. They may not be as pretty but at least they won't kill you."

Reluctantly, Lumpy took Ewewyrd's advice, sauntering over to a patch of very drab puffballs with the consistency of phlegm. He plucked a specimen, eyeing the tiny morsel with disdain before popping it in his mouth. It tasted good so he grabbed another, then two more, and before long he was scooping up handfuls and wolfing them down. Ewewyrd, Kyle and Megan found a patch of their own and joined in the feast.

They moved on after gorging themselves, stumbling upon a footpath that seemed to lead to where they were going and following it through the foothills until darkness forced them to hold up for the night. In the morning they continued along the same path, but eventually lost sight of it as the ground became strewn with rocks thrown off by the sheer, barren peaks. Steam hissed and rose from deep crevices in the ground, making the air around them unpleasantly hot and humid. They were entering Muspelheim; realm of fire.

The trekking was hard, because not only did they have to wind their way up and down rugged serpentine valleys, but they had to do so while they were bone tired. And no one was more exhausted than Kyle. However, as much as he wanted to stop and rest his weary bones, he knew that time was rapidly becoming his worst enemy. With the hood up to keep away curious eyes, he quietly prayed for the strength he needed to keep going, and for a while it seemed like his prayers had been answered. That was before he had to scale a painfully long slope. By the time he reached the level clearing at the top his tank was running on empty. As the world around him went fuzzy, he swayed slightly, clasped a hand to his forehead and fell with a thud to the ground.

Megan screamed and rushed to his side. She shrieked again when she rolled him over and noticed the dark blotches on his neck and under his chin. Sweat was pouring out from underneath the hood so she lowered it, bunching it up and turning it into a makeshift pillow. As she eased the cloak open she saw that the skin it concealed was completely black. And the ring, which used to be a thing of beauty, revealed only a sliver of gold. The remaining gold sparkled as a tear splashed on the ring.

Kyle moaned, dispelling her worse fears. She looked up at Lumpy with beseeching eyes.

"Is there nothing we can do to make it easier for him?"

"I wish there was," said Lumpy, "but even if I remove the ring and take it the rest of the way myself, it won't matter. Only Kyle himself can undo the curse." His ruddy, quivering jowls sagged forlornly. "The best thing we can do now is to let him rest. But first we need to make sure he's more comfortable."

He spotted a rectangular slab pushed up out of the ground like someone had placed it there on purpose. The earth near the base of the standing stone was less pebbly than the surrounding terrain, so Lumpy swept Kyle up in his powerful arms and carried him across to it.

Megan waited for Lumpy to lower Kyle into position before kneeling down and mopping the sweat from his brow and brushing back his greasy hair.

"Come on, Ewewyrd. Kyle doesn't need all three of us to watch over him. Let's you and I look for something to eat."

The elf gave a cry of pain as Lumpy slapped a heavy hand on his aching shoulder.

·　　　·　　　·　　　·

Megan had no idea how long it had been since Lumpy and Ewewyrd went off in search of food but she knew it was long enough for Kyle to recover some of his strength and for her to start worrying about what happened to them. Deep fret lines marred her delicate features.

Kyle was sitting now with his back propped up against the rock. He noticed the concern on Megan's face and said, "I feel much better already so why don't we go and look for them?"

He started to rise but Megan placed a restraining hand on his shoulder.

"That isn't necessary. They'll be back soon. You'll see."

She forced a smile, but Kyle could see by the doubt in her eyes that she didn't believe this for a minute. She lowered her eyelids so he wouldn't be able to read her thoughts.

Kyle leaned back and tried to relax but he had too much on his mind. Becoming increasingly restless, he was going to suggest that he alone go in search of Lumpy and Ewewyrd when a hulking figure appeared in the clearing, grinning from ear to ear.

"Look what I found," said Lumpy in a loud voice. He proudly held up a pea green egg slightly larger than an ostrich egg.

The mountains resounded with his stentorian voice. Distant ears were alerted to the sudden sound.

Megan jumped to her feet, staring in horror at the egg.

"You fool! Do you know what that is?"

Lumpy regarded her oddly. "It's an egg."

"Of course it's an egg, sponge brain! But what kind of egg…"

She was cut short by a tremendous roar that hurt her ears and turned the blood in her veins to ice. A moment later an enormous, terrifying-looking dragon rounded a mountain peak and glided into view. The dragon took one look at the intruders and roared again, beating the air with its leathery, bat-like wings.

Kyle, Megan and Lumpy did the only thing they could do; they ran for their lives. But even running full out they were no match for the aerial monster. It closed in rapidly, fixing its evil, yellow eyes on them.

"Over here," shouted Ewewyrd, waving at them from atop a rocky ledge. A dark gap in the mountain side indicated that he was standing at the entrance to a small cave.

The ledge was too far away to simply leg it out so they split up to give the dragon more to think about. While Megan cut to the left and Lumpy cut to the right, Kyle kept going straight.

The dragon was so close Kyle could feel its hot breath gusting on to the back of his neck. He heard it snort and knew that any second now the monster was going to open its gaping jaws and envelop him in flames, reducing him to cinders. In desperation, he put on a burst of speed and dove over what looked like a plain stone coffin just as the dragon released a jet of fire.

A torrent of flames shot past him, scorching the rocky sarcophagus and licking at his cloak. As the dragon whooshed by, screeching angrily because it had missed its target, he rolled onto his back to smother the flames threatening to devour the cloak. Then he scrambled to his feet. His head pounding, he sprinted for the ledge while the monster circled high in the sky and prepared to strike again. Ewewyrd helped pull him to safety as a second deadly burst strafed the ground behind him.

From just inside the cave Kyle watched the dragon swoop repeatedly, breathing fire and baking the surface until it glowed fiery orange. Looking across the scorched patch of earth he noticed that Lumpy and Megan were trapped, cut off by a sea of molten rock. He wondered why the dragon hadn't finished them off long ago. Then he remembered the egg and it gave him an idea. He stepped out onto the ledge and yelled across to Lumpy.

"Hey, Lumpy, have you still got that egg you showed me?"

"It's right here," said Lumpy, raising the oval-shaped egg like a quarterback aiming to throw a football.

As soon as the dragon saw the egg it let out a panicked squeal and dropped like a bolt of lightning. It struck the ground with a thud, setting off a minor avalanche.

Kyle had to duck inside the cave as tons of dislodged boulders rumbled down the side of the mountain, crashing onto the ground below and exploding in a cloud of dust.

Through the settling dust the dragon loomed large; its green snakelike scales shining evilly in the weak cavern light, its crocodilian mouth stretched in a hideous grin, its deep penetrating eyes glued to Lumpy and the precious egg.

To say Lumpy was petrified would have been an understatement. Yet, there was something about the way the dragon regarded him that suggested he was safe as long as no harm came to the egg. Bearing this in mind, he cradled the egg in his arms and began to make his way to the ledge by slowly side-stepping around the monster. The dragon turned with him, watching his every move. His blood ran cold.

Time seemed to stand still as Lumpy inched his way closer and closer to the ledge. At one point he saw a flash of white and realized that Megan had just run out from behind a rock. Silent as a fleeting shadow, she leapt over and sprinted around the fallen rocks. The dragon took no notice when Kyle reached down and pulled her to safety. It kept its threatening eyes fixed on Lumpy.

There was so much snorting, heavy breathing and crunching of rocks underfoot that Lumpy failed to hear a distinct cracking sound. It wasn't until a second, sharper crack reached his ear that he glanced down and saw a tiny snout peeking through a hole in the egg. The snout disappeared momentarily then reappeared along with a mouth lined with two rows of fearsome little teeth and a pair of evil yellow eyes. The miniature dragon looked from Lumpy to its mother and croaked piteously. With that one pathetic cry he felt the chill of fear clear to the bone.

Lumpy's first instinct was to run but before he fled he tossed the egg high in the air.

The dragon's look of undisguised menace turned to outrage. However, with the diminutive monster trapped inside the eggshell and croaking to beat the band, the distressed mother had to let Lumpy go. Unfurling her bat-like wings, she sprang into the air and caught the little green fiend in one of her huge, scythe-like claws just as it burst out of the casing. The empty eggshell fell away and hit the ground with a splat.

Once the baby was safely set down on the ground, the angry mother set her sights on the ledge and Lumpy's rather large backside, which was just that moment being heaved up onto the platform. Roaring and snorting, the dragon released a jet of fire that skimmed the surface and shot up the rocky ledge, singeing the scrabbling boy's pants. The dragon screeched furiously as Lumpy scuttled inside the cave on all fours, waves of smoke rising from his rear end.

The dragon charged at the ledge, roaring and spitting fire. It continued the barrage, dousing the cave with fire, until it ran out of fuel to feed the flames.

On a nearby mountain peak watchful eyes saw the commotion and, with a single horn blast, a message was relayed deep into the heart of Darkalfheim.

16
DARKALFHEIM

ROARING FIREBALLS ILLUMINATED the cave, baking the shallow cavity until it was hotter than an oven and chasing Kyle and his companions down a narrow slit of a tunnel.

"Hurry up!" pleaded Lumpy, shoving Megan from behind.

"I'm going as fast as I can," shrieked Megan.

The passage they stumbled upon was a mixed blessing. While it allowed them to avoid the immediate threat, it left them with no other means of escape. So, should the fault line, for that's what it really was, end abruptly, their fate would be no different had they stayed put and faced the dragon's wrath. They would be incinerated all the same. But until that time came, until there was no hope at all, they were determined to keep one step ahead of the surging heat.

"That's not what I wanted to hear," Lumpy yelped, as the intense heat licked at his back, vaporizing the sweat seeping through his shirt.

Kyle heard the desperation in Lumpy's voice and he would have liked to speed up but, no matter what his senses told him, his legs refused to listen. It was as though they had suddenly turned to lead and, with every step he took, the weight of them increased until he could do little more than grasp the sides of the tunnel and pull himself along. Where the abrasive surface tore at his rotting flesh, splotches of blood and flakes of dead black skin glistened in his wake.

He was about to collapse, crumple under his own weight, when the walls opened up to reveal a much larger cave. There were two similarly hewn passages, set side by side in the wall, at the far end of the cavern.

The discovery couldn't have come at a more opportune time. No sooner had Kyle and Ewewyrd stepped into the vast chamber than Megan and Lumpy bolted out of the tunnel and yanked them aside. With their backs against the cavern wall, they watched in horror as a jet of hot air shot past them, whooshing fiercely and fanning outward in blistering waves. Luckily the cave was large enough to disperse the heat, so by the time the first wave swept over them it had lost much of its sting.

It reminded Kyle of a sauna, oppressively hot and stuffy. He breathed in greedily to nourish his starving lungs but the air he swallowed contained very little oxygen. His head began to spin and he dropped to one knee.

"Are you alright?" asked Lumpy. He took hold of Kyle's arm to keep him from falling flat on his face.

Lumpy's voice sounded far-away in Kyle's ear.

"I'm fine," he said, brushing aside Lumpy's hand.

Too stubborn to admit the truth, Kyle leaned against the wall and eased himself up off the floor. He managed to take a few tentative steps before his legs wobbled violently and he collapsed face down. He lay still for a moment, then rolled onto his back and looked past Megan's angry glare at the glittering rocks that lined the roof and walls of the cavern. The clear crystals radiated enough dim light to illuminate the spacious chamber.

"You don't look fine," said Megan critically, as she took hold of his arm and gave it a not so gentle tug.

"To tell you the truth I feel terrible."

Kyle slouched forward, resting his forearms on his knees and hanging his head as if the weight was too much to bear. But it was nothing compared to the heaviness he felt in his heart. He had let everyone down, his parents, his friends, the Goblin King and, now, it would appear, he was going to let himself down as well. His body hunched further.

Megan regarded the disfigured, scarred hands suspended limply between Kyle's bent legs with a combination of pity and revulsion. While the constant discharge of blood and pus from the innumerable open wounds cried out for attention, it was the stench of putrefaction deep inside that made her stomach heave and prevented her from doing more than offer a few words of encouragement.

"I know how you must feel Kyle—" As soon as the words left her mouth she realized the absurdity of what she had just said. She saw the pain in his eyes and she knew she couldn't possibly know how he felt, but she continued nonetheless. "—but you mustn't give up hope. Even if it's the only thing that keeps you going, at least it's better than nothing."

Kyle squeezed his eyes shut to hold back the tears that threatened to escape. His voice trembled as he said, "I know you mean well, but I'm too tired and too sore to go any further." He swallowed hard, waiting until he had gained control of his emotions before uttering what he saw as the inevitable. "You three go on without me and leave me here to die in peace."

He grasped the heavy chain that had been digging into his neck for days and tried to remove it. A sickening sucking sound rose from a tacky welt beneath the metal links.

"Nonsense!" said Lumpy, lunging forward and slapping at Kyle's fumbling fingers. "I told you before I would carry you if I had to and that's exactly what I intend to do, as soon as that serpent is through blowing off steam." He paused to take in their surroundings. "Until then, I suggest we stay here where it's safe."

Ewewyrd jumped back as a cloud of hot vapor whooshed through the opening, singeing his eyebrows.

"But what if that monster refuses to leave?"

Lumpy wetted his fingers to douse a spark that had flared up on a single strand of hair sticking up on Ewewyrd's balding head.

"As soon as it realizes we're not stupid enough to step outside it'll get bored and go away."

But the dragon was in no hurry to leave. Not when there was the prospect of an easy meal only a hiccup and a breath away. It lay near the ledge for well over an hour, patiently watching the cave for signs of life. Once in a while its eyes wandered to the little green monster gnawing playfully on its tail, issuing a stern warning when the fiend got carried away, but for the most part keeping its evil yellow eyes fixed on the depression in the side of the mountain.

Lumpy stood in the shadows just inside the cave, listening to the little monster squawk and cursing their bad luck. Soon the entire mountain range was going to be shrouded in darkness and they would have no choice but to hold up for the night. He wasn't looking forward to sitting around doing nothing while his best friend faded away right before his eyes. He had to think of something fast, perhaps a distraction to lure the dragon away from the cave. However, even before the little grey cells inside his head had time to get warm a familiar scream shattered his concentration. Muttering to himself, he slipped inside the tunnel, wondering what on earth Megan was screeching about now.

When he emerged a moment or so later Lumpy found Megan standing alone. Clearly distressed, she was mouthing her hand, nursing a gash.

"What happened to you?" he asked.

"He bit me," she spat, taking her hand away from her mouth and holding it out so that he could see the evidence for himself.

Lumpy stared in disbelief at the bite mark. Blood was oozing from a spot where the teeth had punctured the skin.

"Who did? Kyle?"

"No, Ewewyrd."

"And I thought I was hungry."

Megan clicked her tongue in annoyance and swatted him on the shoulder with the back of her good hand.

"He wasn't trying to make a meal out of me. He was trying to steal the ring."

Lumpy gazed at her in disbelief. "Why would he want to do that?"

"It beats me. I was asleep so I didn't see or hear a thing. Not until Ewewyrd tripped over my foot. He had the ring in one hand and a guilty look on his face. One glance and I knew he was up to no good." She paused to lap up some blood.

Lumpy twisted his face in disgust.

"Is that really necessary?"

"It is, unless you want me to bleed all over myself."

"That might not be such a bad idea," said Lumpy blanching. "You're beginning to turn my stomach."

Megan dropped her arm in a huff, pressing her bloody hand against her pants, hoping to stem the flow.

"Anyhow," she said to continue where she left off, "I grabbed the ring and asked him what he was doing. That's when he sank his teeth into me and I screamed. I let go and he fled down that tunnel over there." She pointed to the passage on the left.

"What about Kyle?"

Tears clouded Megan's eyes. "I tried to stop him but he was delirious. He pushed me aside and ran after Ewewyrd. Only, he went the wrong way."

Lumpy mulled things over in his head for a moment but nothing he came up with made much sense. It was totally out of character for

Ewewyrd to take the ring and even more uncharacteristic of him to use force and bite Megan.

"I don't know what Ewewyrd is up to but we have to find them both and bring them back here before it's too late. Do you think you can handle our slippery elf friend now that you know he bites?"

Megan furrowed her brows.

"If he tries that stunt again I'll wring his scrawny neck."

"Good."

With no time to lose, Lumpy dashed across to the tunnel on the right and disappeared inside. Meanwhile, Megan headed for the tunnel on the left, keen to lay her hands on the renegade elf.

•   •   •   •

With a will born of desperation Kyle sped through the rambling passage, chasing shadows and fleeing from the demon that was intent on pursuing him. It kept calling out to him in a devilishly, sweat voice but he refused to listen. In his mind's eye he saw the tainted ring, the one clear image in his confused, troubled mind. It was so much a part of him he felt incomplete without it wrapped around his neck, and the only thing he could focus on was getting it back. Ignoring the pain that was driving him mad, he shed the heavy cloak that had been slowing him down and ran for a beam of light at the end of the tunnel.

He came to a vast open space in the core of the mountain, divided in two by a deep fissure that ran down the centre. Magma bubbled near the surface of the crevice, flowing under a natural stone bridge and filling the cavern with its warm glow. As he scanned his surroundings he saw Ewewyrd dart out of a nearby tunnel. The ring, his precious ring, was clenched in the thieving elf's fist. He peered at the culprit with unveiled hostility.

"How could you?" said Kyle, startling Ewewyrd.

Ewewyrd halted, panting and gazing wide-eyed at Kyle. His chest tightened as he was overcome with guilt and, for a moment, he thought about returning the ring. Then he noticed the crevice and the steam rising from the magma within and he knew he had to go through with his plan, regardless of the outcome. His eyes flitted from the fissure, to Kyle and back to the fissure again.

Kyle must have sensed what Ewewyrd was going to do because as soon as the elf moved, making a beeline for the crevice, he rushed forward and tackled him. As he felt his legs fall out from under him Ewewyrd shrieked; a high, thin keening sound like a rabbit caught in a snare. He hit the ground with a thud, expelling what little air was left in his lungs and releasing the ring. It flew away from his groping hands towards the bridge.

They scrambled to retrieve the ring, pulling and clawing at each other like two slobbering, crazed beasts. Eventually, Kyle grabbed onto the chain first, using his longer reach to gain the upper hand. However, no sooner had he taken hold of it than his head exploded and it slipped through his senseless fingers. Ewewyrd dropped the rock he had clunked Kyle over the head with and sprung to his feet. To his dismay, he found himself staring at Lumpy's ugly mug.

"What are you trying to do? Kill him!"

Megan burst onto the scene a moment later, saw Kyle lying in a crumbled heap, and thought Ewewyrd had indeed done him in.

"How could you?" she said, crying out in horror.

She rushed over to Kyle's side and collapsed, tears streaming down her bloodless cheeks. As if to lessen her anguish, the supposed corpse uttered a pained moan when a teardrop plopped on his nose.

"What does it matter?" said Ewewyrd. "He's going to die anyway."

Lumpy noted the frenetic look in Ewewyrd's eyes and he knew he was dealing with a troubled mind. He resolved to make his move before the deranged elf did anything else he would live to regret.

"Not if I have anything to say about it," he said, lunging at Ewewyrd.

In a flash Ewewyrd produced a knife, stabbing at Lumpy's outstretched hand.

Startled, Lumpy jumped back. He gazed in disbelief at the deep gash painting his left hand red.

"Have you gone mad?"

"Mad!" screeched Ewewyrd, foaming at the mouth like a rabid dog. "Of course I'm mad. I've been mad all my life. Only there wasn't much I could do about it. There wasn't much any of us could do about it. The goblins made all the rules. The lesser elves had to listen. Listen and obey. Obey or else." He spat to show his disdain for the goblins who had ruled over his people for so long. "I hate them for turning us into slaves. I hate them for making us always live in fear. And I hate this—this—ring even more."

Flakes of blackened metal sprinkled to the ground as he held up the ring—Draupner—and shook it violently.

"It was the gold from this ring and everything the goblins were able to acquire with it that gave them so much power. Before they possessed it they were no better than us. The ring changed everything, but not any more."

Lumpy edged closer but Ewewyrd backed away, wielding the knife in a threatening manner.

"Don't try anything stupid," he warned. "I'm going to destroy the ring if it's the last thing I do."

"Ewewyrd!"

Not only Ewewyrd, but Lumpy and Megan jumped at the sound of the booming voice. Ewewyrd shifted slightly so he could keep one eye on Lumpy and, through the other eye, he saw King Bruide standing large on the other side of the fissure. He was surrounded by a handful of his own men and two wizened, misshapen dwarves that looked as surly and grim-faced as Brokk; the dark elves of Darkalfheim.

The king stepped forward out of the crowd.

"I believe you have something that rightfully belongs to me," he said in a calm manner.

Ewewyrd gave a dry, humorless laugh.

"Not any more your Highness. It's mine now and I'll do with it what I please." Contempt laced his voice.

"Oh. And when, pray tell, did I give the ring to you?"

The king saw Lumpy creeping towards Ewewyrd and shot him a warning glance. Lumpy froze.

"The moment it came into my possession," said Ewewyrd with a sneer.

King Bruide's expression hardened.

"Look, elf! Give me the ring and I'll forget all about this terrible misunderstanding." He held out his hand and moved towards the bridge.

"Never!"

Ewewyrd ran for the fissure but was forced to stop short when an arrow hit the ground in front of him. In the meantime, King Bruide proceeded to cross the bridge.

"You don't understand," the king said in a return to persuasive calmness. "I don't want the ring so I can make more gold. I want to destroy it just like you."

Ewewyrd shook with rage.

"Liar! Why would you want to do that?"

"To break the curse and save Kyle's life."

Ewewyrd scoffed at the idea.

"You expect me to believe that. What do you think I am, a fool?"

"You are if you don't listen. Now, give—me—the—ring."

Ewewyrd noticed that the king was advancing towards him as he spoke. Afraid that he was getting too close, Ewewyrd made a sudden movement and, once again, an arrow landed at his feet. Bearing his teeth in a grim smile he stomped on the barbed head, snapping the arrow in two and almost daring the archer to do better.

The archer notched another arrow as Ewewyrd moved closer to the fissure.

"Wait!" shouted Megan.

Ewewyrd came to the bridge and paused, glancing down at the fiery, orange river. He was so close to the edge all he had to do was drop the ring and watch his troubles dissolve. Suddenly bereft of courage, his legs began to shake and his lips to quiver. The ring began to flake even more in his trembling hand.

"For heaven's sake, Ewewyrd, listen to what he has to say," pleaded Megan.

King Bruide crept closer, careful not to startle Ewewyrd. He was so close now he could almost reach out and touch the troubled elf.

"I know you don't believe me but it's true. The only way to break the curse is to destroy the ring. But the only one who can do that is me. And I have to do so willingly."

He extended his hand in what looked like an act of friendship; something Ewewyrd had never seen him do before, to anyone, especially not a lowly elf.

Ewewyrd gazed into the king's eyes and saw something else he had never seen before; compassion, understanding, remorse. Shaking uncontrollably, he reached out and placed the crumbling ring in the king's outstretched hand.

The king saw hope flare in the elf's tearful eyes and smiled warmly as she said, "You won't regret this, Ewewyrd." Then he held the crumbling ring over the lava bath and let it fall from his hand. Ewewyrd watched wide-eyed as it drifted through a cloud of steam and splashed into the searing river. It floated on the surface for a moment, sizzling and giving off a foul odor before being gobbled up by the molten rock.

•　　　•　　　•　　　•

Three days later Kyle, who had been gravely ill even before Ewewyrd whacked him on the head, began to show signs of improvement. The first indication that he was on the mend came when he woke with a start from a deep sleep the day after King Bruide had destroyed the ring. He asked for a glass of water to sooth his parched throat. Then he immediately went back to sleep and didn't stir again until the following morning, with an appetite, as well as, a thirst.

As the second day progressed he became more alert and talkative and, in-between naps, he chatted with Lumpy, Megan and Jan, or anyone else who happened to drop by to see how the patient was doing. By nighttime, much of the natural color had returned to his body; only his hands remained severely discolored and tender.

Finally, on the morning of the third day, he was growing irritated with his own inability to move about as freely as he would have liked and, sensing his impatience, King Bruide declared him fit to go and preparations were made to depart.

The announcement was greeted with cheers, by everyone who was anxious to leave, and just as enthusiastically by the host dark elves, who would have cheered louder if only the departure hadn't been postponed until after the midday meal. There was barely enough food to go around at the best of times, and even less with the likes of King Bruide and Lumpy to please.

With mixed feelings, the master chef raided the larder one last time and laid his hands on enough food to cook up a meal fit for a king. By all accounts, it was the finest meal he had prepared in a long time, even if every man, woman and child was going to have to draw their belt tighter as a result.

And to emphasize just how tight they would have to pull King Bruide gave a satisfied belch as he extended a greasy hand to his host. "Thank you again, Sindri."

Bandy-legged and squat, gnarled and seamed with age, the dark elf leader, Sindri the Wise, took the proffered hand, squinting through bleary eyes at the small crowd gathered outside one of the many entrances to Darkalfheim's dark and secretive world. Its warren of tunnels and chambers were a mystery to all but the inhabitants.

"Godspeed, King Bruide. And don't forget to give my regards to that rascal Brokk. If he eats as much as you say he does, it's a good thing you didn't bring him with you."

The king rested a bloated hand on his bulging stomach and felt a pang of guilt for overindulging himself at the expense of his host, whose gaunt features were in sharp contrast to his own.

"Rest assured, Sindri, that your hospitality will not go unrewarded. I've already made plans to send you a dozen ewes in foal." As an afterthought he added, "And a dozen more fit for the slaughter."

Sindri licked his lips in anticipation and cackled.

"Just you make sure you do, your Highness. Just you make sure you do."

With nothing more to add he turned his back on the king and his party, leaving them to find their own way home.

King Bruide grimaced as he was reminded of Brokk. Like father, like son, he thought to himself as he watched the aged dwarf hobble away, still cackling as he vanished through a barely noticeable slit in the mountainside.

The king had one last thing to take care of before they departed and it had to do with Ewewyrd. He saw the elf standing nervously next to Megan and shouted out his name.

Ewewyrd started in surprise, still not accustomed to hearing the Goblin King call him by his name. He asked Megan to pinch him to make sure he wasn't dreaming.

She refused. Instead, she drew him closer and hugged him fondly.

"Take care of yourself, Ewewyrd."

She kissed him on the forehead and released him.

His cheeks flaming with embarrassment, Ewewyrd staggered to Lumpy and held out his puny hand.

Once again Lumpy had managed to stuff himself on the rich, exotic fare prepared for his pleasure and his innards were just now venting their anger. He gazed glassy-eyed at Ewewyrd's hand, sweat prickling his forehead, a pallid sheen to his skin.

Fearful that Lumpy was going to barf on him, Ewewyrd muttered a quick, "good-bye", and hastened over to Kyle.

Given the gravity of his injuries, the king arranged to have a litter constructed during the three days that Kyle had been convalescing. And now, as Ewewyrd look down at the pathetic, sickly youth sprawled out on the makeshift carrier, he was saddened by the fact that his actions had led to more grief for the one person who had already been through enough. The trembling lips and puffy eyes were testimony of his unhappiness.

Kyle saw the look of guilt on Ewewyrd's face and he tried to reassure the elf that all was forgotten.

"I don't blame you for what you did. Who knows, I might have done the same thing. It's enough to know you're truly sorry."

He endeavored to sit up but it was either too painful or he was just too weak. He fell back, grimacing and grunting at having made the effort.

Ewewyrd gave a strained smile.

"Thank you for understanding," he said, reaching down to gently squeeze Kyle's bandaged hand. "And thank you too," he said to Jan, sitting astride the beast that was hitched to the litter.

If it hadn't been for Jan, the king would have never arrived in time to save Kyle. Jan offered Ewewyrd her hand and he gave it a tender squeeze, as well.

Feeling much better about things now that he knew how Kyle felt, Ewewyrd stepped more lightly as he finally approached the king.

Having waited for Ewewyrd to make his farewells King Bruide was ready to start making good on his promise. With the elf standing at attention before him, still somewhat in awe of his greatness, the king announced loud and clear so that everyone could hear, "A person can be blinded by too much gold. When that happens it takes someone special to come along and open your eyes so you can see clearly." He glanced at Jan, an appreciative smile on his face. Then he placed an encouraging hand on Ewewyrd's shoulder and continued. "I know I can't change the past, but I can certainly help shape the future. And when we return to Midgard, I promise you that the future will be brighter for you and all the elves."

Ewewyrd had never felt happier. Everything he had ever wished for, everything he had ever dreamed about was finally going to come true. He felt like jumping up and down, screaming for joy, but before he was able to make a complete fool of himself the king clapped his hands, stirring him from his reverie and making his ears ring.

He watched as one of the riders broke from the pack and rode towards him. Although his ears were still ringing he heard the king say, "I know you left some unfinished business behind in Alfheim and this fine fellow is going to make sure you arrive there safely to take care of it."

Overwhelmed by the king's generosity and the prospect of seeing Freyja again, Ewewyrd could say or do nothing as the horse halted next to him and a massive hand hoisted his numb body up off the ground and plunked him down onto the saddle. As the horse lurched forward, he threw his arms around the rider's back and gripped the folds of his tunic.

Tears of joy and sadness ran down his cheeks as they rode away and he waved farewell to his four human friends. He left them knowing that their paths would never cross again, not in this or any other world. But then, stranger things have happened.

Epilogue

In a beam of cavern sunshine that lit up the clearing, the same patch of ground Kyle and his companions had stumbled upon during the first night of their journey, the nymph, Saffron, came into view. Striding gracefully alongside her was the most beautiful creature Kyle had ever had the pleasure of observing; a legendary unicorn. One glimpse and he was enamored by its beauty.

The filtered light that peeked through the dense canopy reflected off the majestic creature's flawless white coat, illuminating the clearing and the bystanders gathered in the shadows. Saffron extended her arms, coaxing one of the onlookers forward with a winning smile and a gentle wave of her hands.

Jan advanced, cautiously at first, then more boldly as the unicorn bowed its head in submission, allaying her fears. When she was no more than a foot away she reached out and touched the placid creature, gently stroking its velvety lower jaw. A feeling of warmth and well-being coursed through her veins.

She gazed into the large oval eyes, clearing her mind of all those frivolous thoughts that saturate one's brain and letting the unicorn see beyond life's petty worries, inside her very soul. Before long the creature's eyes clouded over and the first tears began to form.

Jan raised her right left hand and, with the other hand, she removed the glass stopper from a crystal vial she had brought along with her. Then she placed the bottle just below one of the unicorn's watery eyes to catch the precious teardrops as they began to fall. Within minutes, the vial was almost full and the steady stream quickly slowed to a trickle. Not wanting to miss a drop, Jan held the bottle in place.

The unicorn kicked at the ground with one hind leg, indicating that her time was up.

Jan waited to capture one last drop before she repositioned the stopper and tapped it into place. Then she kissed the unicorn's snout and said, "thank you."

The unicorn whinnied and shook its head at her as if to say, "your welcome."

Clasping the vial to her heart, Jan strolled across the clearing to where Kyle was sitting on the ground with his back propped up against a tree. She recalled how dark and blotchy his complexion had been shortly after the ring was destroyed, and she was amazed by how quickly the color had returned to normal. But that was the extent of his recovery. Somehow, the cancer inside was more insidious than first thought and despite the initial optimism his condition was progressively getting worse. Not wanting him to suffer any longer, Jan unplugged the vial and handed him the bottle, with the firm belief that the contents would reverse the damage and finally undo the lasting effects of the curse.

For his part, Kyle had heard more than enough in recent days about the unicorn's ability to heal and much that reached his ears was just too fanciful to believe. Was it any wonder then when he hesitated, gazing at the cloudy solution through doubtful eyes?

"Drink it!" ordered Jan, frowning severely at him just like their mother did when she refused to take her medicine.

"Alright," said Kyle relenting. "But I really don't see what good it will do."

He sniffed the solution. Then he tested it with his tongue. There was a slight tingling sensation where the brackish liquid was absorbed. Realizing that everyone was staring at him, eagerly awaiting the results, he tipped back the bottle.

As the solution slid down his throat he was overwhelmed by the same feelings of warmth and well-being that Jan had experienced and, even before he was through draining half the bottle, he could feel the magical elixir coursing through his veins, flushing out the corruption and bringing renewed strength to every fiber of his body. Within minutes he had amassed so much energy he knew he had to do something for fear of exploding. Much to everyone's surprise he sprang to his feet, bouncing up and down like a March hare, overjoyed by the prospect of new life. It took the king to bring him back down to earth.

"You better put the stopper on that before you spill it and there's nothing left for your father."

Kyle stared in horror at the vial, fearful that some of the elixir may have slopped out while he was prancing around like a fool. Luckily, the bottle was still more than half full. He promptly pushed the stopper down, gripping the vial tightly and holding it close to his heart, just as Jan had done. While it wasn't quite the treasure of his dreams, it was all that he had hoped for and worth more to him than gold. Tears of joy ran down his cheeks as he thought of his sick father and all the happy moments still to come.

King Bruide read his mind and placed a proud hand on Kyle's shoulder.

"Someday I would like to have a son of my own and, when that day comes, I hope he loves me just as much as you love your father, Kyle Dunlap."